COMMONWEALTH OF PENNSYLVANIA
ESEA TITLE II, 19 73

Please return to:
Aquinas Academy Library
2308 W. Hardies Road
Gibsonia, PA 15044
724-444-0722

Papa's Secret Chocolate Dessert

Illustrated by
LILIAN OBLIGADO

AMALIE SHARFMAN
Papa's Secret Chocolate Dessert

Lothrop, Lee & Shepard Company

NEW YORK

By Amalie Sharfman

Papa's Secret Chocolate Dessert
Mr. Peabody's Pesky Ducks
A Beagle Named Bertram

Text copyright © 1972 by Amalie Sharfman
Illustrations copyright © 1972 by Lilian Obligado

All rights reserved. No part of this book may be reproduced or utilized in any form or by any means, electronic or mechanical, including photocopying, recording or by any information storage and retrieval system, without permission in writing from the Publisher. Inquiries should be addressed to Lothrop, Lee and Shepard Company, 105 Madison Ave., New York, N.Y. 10016.
Printed in the United States of America.
Library of Congress Catalog Card Number: 77-177319

to Carrie M. Stern and Henry S. Stern
two of the best chefs I have ever known

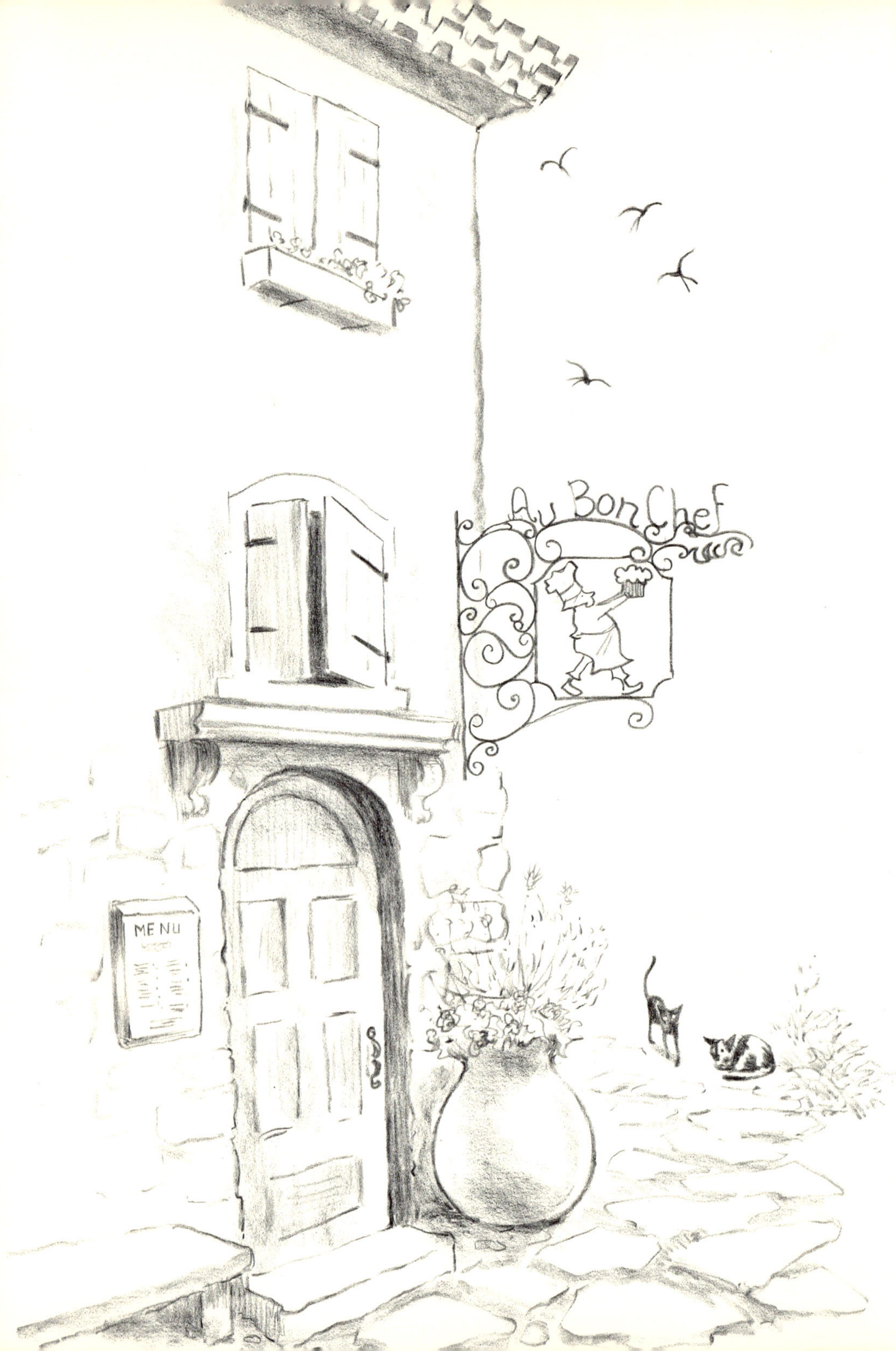
Au Bon Chef
MENU

Jean-Pierre Chardin and his family lived over a restaurant in a village in the south of France. The restaurant was owned by Jean-Pierre's father, Monsieur Henri Chardin, who was also the chef. He was such a fine chef that people came from far and wide to taste his cooking.

Now that it was summer, and there was no school, Jean-Pierre could sleep as long as he liked. Today, as soon as he woke up, he sensed that it was late. Nine o'clock at least, he guessed. The sun was streaming through his window in a golden flood. The summer breeze was already hot. But even without these signs, his ears and nose would have told him how late it was because of the sounds and smells coming from Papa's kitchen downstairs just below his room. Luncheon preparations must be well under way.

There was the loud, cheerful banging of pots and pans. The clop-clop of the knife on the chopping board. The whirring and stirring of wire whisks, eggbeaters, and spoons. Jean-Pierre knew that these sounds were being made by his two older brothers, Georges and Albert, who were Papa's *sous-chefs,* his kitchen helpers.

There was the delicious smell of cooking—Papa's! Jean-Pierre jumped out of bed, hastily washed, and yanked on his clothes. Smoothing his dark, curly hair with his hands, he ran downstairs to the kitchen.

As he opened the door, Jean-Pierre paused for just a moment and looked around as he always did —as though he were seeing it all for the first time. How much he loved it, Papa's kitchen and everything that went on in it. How beautiful it was, with its red-tiled floor, its huge coal stove, its walls covered with gleaming copper dishes, its jars and tins of spices and seasonings, sugar and flour . . .

But Maman and Papa were having one of their arguments. At once Jean-Pierre knew that it was about him, although as usual they were enjoying themselves so much they didn't even notice that he was there.

Maman's black eyes were sparkling angrily and her hands were pressed firmly to her hips. "He should be out in the fresh air more, that child," she was saying crossly, "instead of spending so much time in this wretched kitchen. He will grow up thin and pale. Haven't you observed how thin and pale he already is? Or is your head so buried in your pots and pans that you can see nothing else?"

"Nonsense," rumbled Papa. He delicately tasted with a large spoon his *Specialité de la Maison,* one of the elegant stews for which he was renowned. "At Jean-Pierre's age they all look like spiders. I have spent my entire life in the kitchen, and did *I* grow up thin and pale?"

"Ha, ha, how you amuse me!" cried Maman,

looking not in the least amused. She glanced over Papa from head to toe. As anyone could plainly see, his face was as red as an apple and his stomach was as round as a pumpkin.

Jean-Pierre was deeply troubled. In just a week he would be ten years old. For as many of those ten years as he could remember, Papa's kitchen had been his favorite place. It would make him sad indeed if he could never stay there again. Maman was thin and wiry and as small-boned as a sparrow. But as Jean-Pierre knew all too well, she was strong and determined, and she usually got what she wanted.

Jean-Pierre crept to the refrigerator and took out the glasses of juice and milk and the U-shaped roll called a *croissant* that Maman had left for him. Quietly he started toward the table, although all at once he wasn't very hungry.

The closing of the refrigerator door, however, made Georges look up from the onions he was mincing. "Well, well," he exclaimed to Albert. "See what the cat dragged in."

Albert put aside his eggbeater and pretended to be surprised. "Ah, a rat, would you say?" he asked Georges. "But no, more the size of a mouse, after all. Although for a mouse he manages to nibble quite a lot of food, don't you think?"

"It's the smallest mouse that makes the greatest hole in the cheese," said Georges wisely, having the last word as usual.

Georges, who was already almost as stout as Papa, bossed Albert around because Albert was two years younger. Albert was thin as a fence post. So he, in turn, liked nothing better than to remind Jean-Pierre of how skinny *he* was. And most of the time, both of them treated Jean-Pierre as though he didn't exist except for them to tease.

Jean-Pierre pretended not to hear them. Long ago he had tried making angry retorts, but that only made Georges and Albert tease the harder. Finally, he had learned to keep quiet and to be as inconspicuous as possible while secretly raging inside himself.

Papa closed the oven door and turned around.

"Ah, hello, good morning, Jean-Pierre," he cried with a welcoming smile. "Maman and I were just talking about you. Maman feels that you should be out in the fresh air more."

"I know," said Jean-Pierre fearfully. He waited for Papa to say the fatal words that would banish him from the kitchen. But Papa had something else on his mind.

"Next Thursday is your birthday, yes?" continued Papa. "What would you say to a new bicycle? Yours is twice as old as you are—Albert rode it first."

For a long time Jean-Pierre had been expecting this question. Even so, he wasn't ready with the answer. He did want a new bicycle badly. In fact there was a very important reason for his wanting one. But he wanted something else even more. The trouble was, he was so afraid that Papa would refuse that after all this time he couldn't make himself ask for it.

When he remained silent, Papa looked puzzled and Maman grew impatient. "What is it, Jean-

Pierre?" she asked sharply. "Here Papa and I offer to get you a brand new bicycle for your birthday, and you look like seven days' rain."

"Don't let him fool you," shouted Albert over the noise of Georges' chopping knife. "He wants one, all right. He told me so only last week. He even said what kind he wanted—a Comet. The most expensive kind, you'll be glad to know. Nothing's too good for our Jean-Pierre!"

"I don't mind the expense for once," said Papa. "It owes us nothing, that ancient bicycle. That's that, then. A Comet it shall be." He turned back to the stove. "Now, where was I?" he asked himself. "Ah, yes. This soup needs a few more onions, and just a dash or two of freshly ground pepper."

Jean-Pierre gave such a sigh that it ruffled the feathers of a chicken lying on a table waiting to be plucked. He still hadn't told Papa what he wanted most of all. When, oh, when would he ever get enough courage?

Maman's voice broke through his gloomy thoughts. "Good. Now that we've settled that problem, Jean-Pierre, there's no reason for you not to go for a nice bicycle ride before lunch."

Taking his time, Jean-Pierre clumped out to the tool shed where he kept his battered old bicycle. He wheeled it out as slowly as possible. He knew that his friend, Claude, would be waiting for him inside the gate that led to the road, just as he had done every morning since school let out.

There he was! Lousy Old Claude, Jean-Pierre secretly called him, or L.O.C. for short, looking as usual as though he owned the world.

Riding at a snail's pace, Jean-Pierre stopped his bicycle next to Claude's. "Hello," he said. "Waiting long?"

"Not really," answered Claude. "My father just raised my allowance to one hundred and twenty centimes, so to celebrate I stopped off at the *pâtisserie* on my way here and got a plum tart. Oh, la la!" Claude rolled his eyes and patted his stomach in fond memory of the tart.

Jean-Pierre's allowance was just half that much, so he made no reply. He had found, as with his

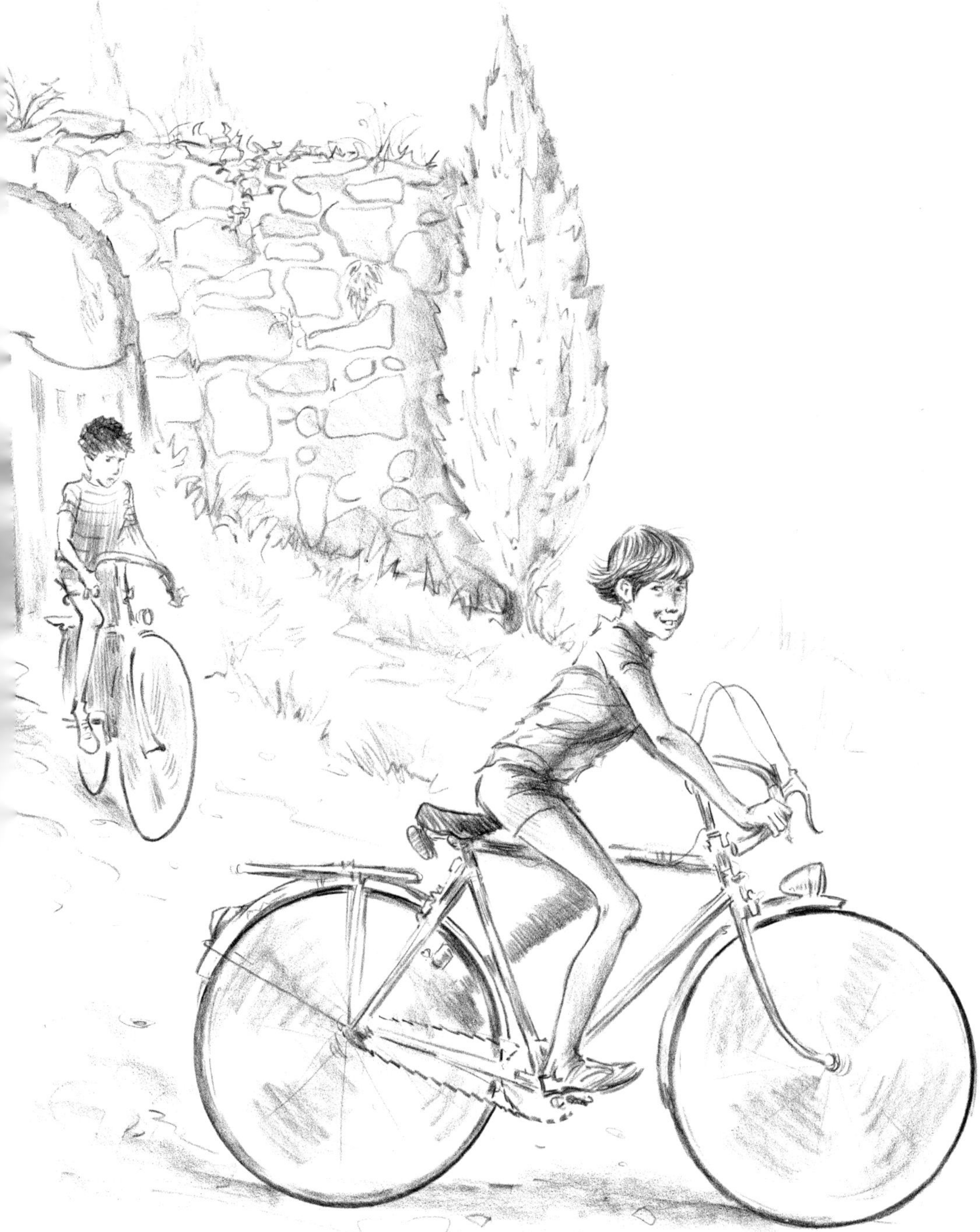

brothers, that silence was often the best weapon for dealing with L.O.C.

But Claude wasn't satisfied. "Know why my allowance was raised?" he asked. "Because my report card was so good. How was yours?"

Jean-Pierre wondered how big a lie to tell. Surely the truth wouldn't do, for he had got only a "five," barely average. Both Maman and Papa had scolded him about it. He decided that a medium-sized lie would be best. "Oh, I got a 'six,' " he said carelessly, as though the matter were of no importance.

"Ah, too bad!" exclaimed Claude. "I got an 'eight.' Better luck next time." And off he rode on his swift, beautiful bicycle—a Comet.

Trailing behind, Jean-Pierre asked himself, as he had so often, why he went on seeing Claude when he so often disliked him. Claude was bright. He was handsome. He was at least two inches taller than Jean-Pierre, and his shoulders were straight and wide. Maman would never call *him* thin and pale. In fact everything Claude did or had seemed better than other people's—including his bicycle.

"Just wait a week, my fine-feathered friend," Jean-Pierre told Claude's faraway back. "Just wait until my birthday. You will not be so high and mighty then!"

Suddenly Claude slowed down so that Jean-Pierre could not help but catch up with him. "Let's ride to the village," he suggested. "I saw a fancy-looking pen and pencil set in one of the shop windows and I want to see how much it is."

Jean-Pierre hesitated. "What time is it?" he asked, glancing at Claude's watch.

" 'What time is it? What time is it?' " mimicked Claude in a disgusted tone. "Every day it's the same thing. We ride for a half hour or an hour at the most, and then you ask what time it is and go home. What's the matter? Does your mother want to know where you are every minute? You must be a bigger baby than I thought!"

Claude was right, Jean-Pierre realized. The truth was that he had a very special reason for wanting to be home by a certain time, and he didn't want to tell Claude, who might try to spoil it for him by laughing or poking fun.

"Well," he said carefully, "I have something to attend to. You know how it is when you have something important to attend to that won't wait."

"Ha!" exclaimed Claude scornfully. "A likely story! What's so important, may I inquire?"

"Ha! yourself," called Jean-Pierre over his shoulder as he pedaled away. "Wouldn't you like to know!"

As he headed toward home, Jean-Pierre felt that he could hardly wait until he got his new Comet. Then at last L.O.C. would have to laugh out of the other side of his mouth! All at once Jean-Pierre forgot Claude completely and remembered why he was in such a hurry to get home at this particular time. Was he too late? Had he taken too long?

He pedaled home as fast as he could, wheeled his bicycle into the shed, ran up the path, and slipped through the back door that led to the kitchen. No! Thank goodness, he was not late. Papa was just beginning to make the chocolate dessert for which he was famous.

Of the many great moments that he spent in Papa's kitchen, to Jean-Pierre this one was always the greatest, and it seemed to him like a miracle each time it happened.

The dessert was called *Chocolat Chardin*. Papa had named it after himself because he had invented it, and no one but he knew the exact recipe. Hundreds of people had eaten it. Everyone tried to discover what made it so much better than any other chocolate dessert they had ever tasted. But no one had been able to solve the mystery, and to this day it remained Papa's secret.

As with each dish that he made, Papa told himself aloud what to do in a mumble so low that Jean-Pierre, who was never more than a foot from the stove, had to strain his ears to hear. "First, we melt the chocolate v-e-r-y slowly," Papa began, putting several squares of chocolate into a small saucepan over a low flame. "Now, we put into the

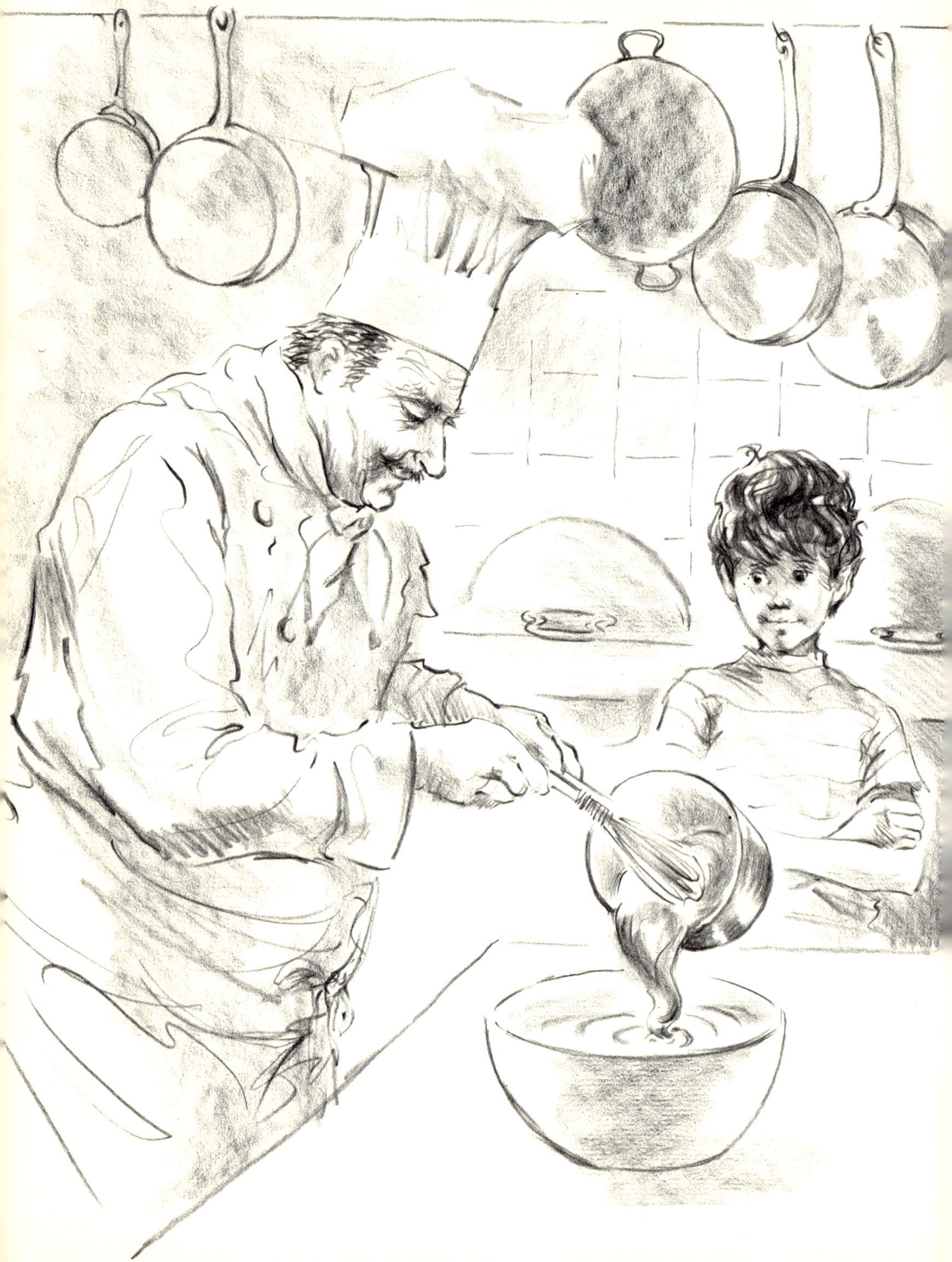

mixing bowl the sugar. *Très bien!* Next, we combine the sugar and egg yolks and beat well. Excellent. And now, let us see about the chocolate. Ah, yes. Just soft enough, I think...."

And so it went, with Papa mumbling and measuring and mixing until he was finished—or almost. For now came what Jean-Pierre called "The Test." The time had come for Papa to decide whether or not this particular *Chocolat Chardin* was as perfect as each and every one of the others he had made.

Jean-Pierre always held his breath while "The Test" was going on. For when the dessert wasn't entirely to his liking, Papa's rage and disappointment were dreadful to behold.

He would roll his eyes toward the ceiling, smack himself a great blow on the forehead, call himself every name he could think of, from "Dirty Pig" to "Stupid Camel," and end by throwing the whole bowlful into the sink. Then, after calming his nerves with a cup of the strong black coffee that he always kept simmering on the stove, he would begin all over again.

Today, though, Papa had no sooner begun "The Test" than Jean-Pierre could tell at once that this *Chocolat* was just right. Papa dipped his little finger into the mixture, tasted it, and cocked his head to one side as though he were listening to something. Then, as he slid it into the oven, he nodded, smiling joyously, and shouted the same words he always did when he was truly satisfied. "*Voilà!* Perfect! The best I've ever made!"

From his corner near the stove Jean-Pierre gazed at Papa with pride. How grand he looked, dressed all in snowy white from his tall chef's hat to his apron that reached almost to the floor. Suddenly Jean-Pierre felt so warm and good inside that he knew this was what people meant when they said, "I have never been so happy."

As the week went by and his birthday drew nearer, Jean-Pierre could scarcely wait to see the look on Claude's face when he, Jean-Pierre, came speeding along on his shiny new Comet.

But far more important, all week Jean-Pierre had been making a plan. Now at last he knew exactly how and when he would ask Papa for the thing he wanted most of all. He had planned so carefully that he had even thought of answers to any objections that Papa or Maman might raise. He was certain now that they would approve in the end.

When Thursday finally arrived, Jean-Pierre was ready. He felt brave and strong. He was sure this would turn out to be the best day of his entire life.

Usually, after all of the luncheon guests had gone, the family ate in the kitchen, enjoying the delicious leftovers from Papa's cooking. Today, though, in honor of Jean-Pierre's birthday, they had lunch in the restaurant. Maman had set the table with a fresh white cloth. Papa had baked a fluffy cheese soufflé. And even Georges and Albert were nice to him for a change. They had joined in the celebration by making Jean-Pierre's favorite tossed salad of lettuce, endive, and romaine.

But this wasn't all. At the very end of the meal Papa left the table, went to the kitchen, and a few moments later returned, carrying high over his head a huge birthday cake blazing with candles.

"Blow out the candles and make a wish!" cried Maman as Papa set the cake in front of Jean-Pierre.

"Only don't say what it is or it won't come true," warned Georges.

"It won't come true if I *don't* say what it is," said Jean-Pierre decisively. The moment he had planned for so carefully had finally arrived. He took a giant breath and blew out all the candles at once. Then in a loud, clear voice he said, "I wish to be a *sous-chef* in Papa's kitchen like Georges and Albert. And I wish it *now!*"

Jean-Pierre's words were followed by complete silence. Anxiously he glanced around the table at their shocked faces. Papa was staring into space, looking as though his thoughts weren't there at all. Was it possible that he hadn't heard?

Suddenly the silence was broken by Albert, and after that everyone had something to add.

"A baby like you be a *sous-chef?*" asked Albert scornfully. "Why, you're hardly dry behind the ears yet."

"But even if you were old enough, how could we use a third *sous-chef* in that cubbyhole of a kitchen?" demanded Georges. "You know that you have to stand in the corner as it is, and even so, there's barely enough room for the rest of us to move around in."

"And what about your schooling?" asked Maman. "Or were you thinking of giving that up?" She turned angrily to Papa. "I could have told you that something like this would happen," she scolded. "Letting him stay in the kitchen so much, he was bound to get ideas. As for the bicycle, we might just as well put it away in the attic for all the use he'll get out of it."

This was the first mention that anyone had made of the bicycle. Jean-Pierre realized with astonishment that in the excitement of revealing his wish, and in his fear, now, that it wasn't going to come true, he had completely forgotten the Comet he had so longed for.

Papa held up his hand like a traffic policeman. "Silence!" he commanded. "Jean-Pierre, did you really think that you could be a *sous-chef* at your age? Surely you have seen how long and hard Georges and Albert work each day. But they are much older than you. They are much stronger. Most important of all, they have finished school. Wanting something is very different from being able to do it. One must face reality in this world."

"But I have!" shouted Jean-Pierre. He was suddenly furious with Papa, who didn't understand, and with Maman and Georges and Albert who didn't want to understand. "Why couldn't I work in the kitchen instead of just watching? In the summer, when there's no school anyway. And in the winter when I come home from school?"

"Work?" asked Georges, his fat cheeks quivering with indignation. "What work, I should like to know? Chopping vegetables? Mixing salad dressing? Making sauces? Albert and I already do all that and more besides, and Papa does the cooking. So what would you do?"

"Except get in the way," muttered Albert.

"All right, then," Jean-Pierre cried quickly. "If I can't be a *sous-chef*, I can be a *sous-sous-chef*."

"A *what*?" asked Papa. "In all my experience I have never heard of a *sous-sous-chef*."

"Don't you see?" Jean-Pierre asked. "Since Georges and Albert are your *sous-chefs* and help you in the kitchen, I could be the *sous-sous-chef* and help them to help you in the kitchen." Jean-Pierre gazed imploringly at Papa, longing for him to understand.

"Aha! Now I see what you mean!" Papa exclaimed. "But it will take you many more years of looking and listening and learning before you are ready to do even so simple a task as peeling a potato in just the right way. I know that you don't believe me now, Jean-Pierre, but someday you will. In spite of the countless meals I've cooked, I still make mistakes. Keep your eyes and ears open every minute that you're in the kitchen, and your time will come."

So that was that, Jean-Pierre told himself bitterly. He hadn't got his dearest wish after all. How stupid to have imagined that he would!

Maman began piling the dishes onto her tray. "And the bicycle?" she asked. "What about that?"

"Bicycle?" asked Papa, his eyes two great round "O's" of confusion. "What bi—yes, yes, of course, *naturellement,* how stupid of me. Well now, the bicycle. Yes, yes. You see, as to that . . ."

As usual, Papa had so lost himself in his world of cooking that everything else was forgotten. Maman pulled him back.

"Henri, don't you recall Jean-Pierre's birthday present?" she asked. "Where we hid it so that he wouldn't see it until today?"

"Ah, to be sure!" exclaimed Papa in relief. "Of course I remember. We hid it behind the tool shed. Come! Let us look at it."

Papa led the way to the shed with the rest of them trailing behind. *"Voilà!"* he cried with a flourish so grand he might have been placing a *Chocolat Chardin* before La Comtesse de Ville.

There it was! It was large and handsome. It was new and shiny. It looked swift and powerful. There was only one thing wrong. It was not a Comet.

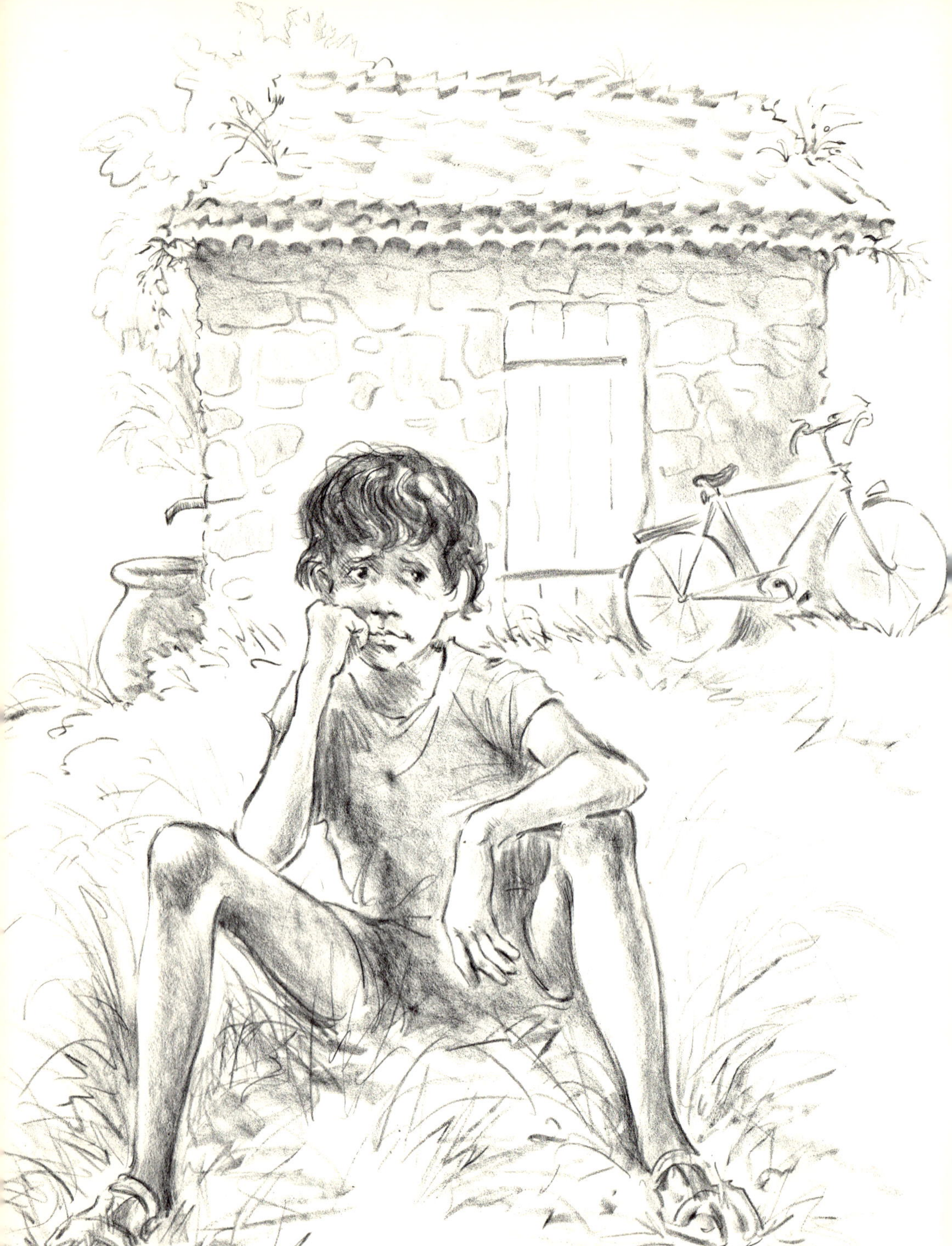

Maman hastened to explain. "We tried, Jean-Pierre, to get you a Comet, because we knew that was the kind of bicycle you wanted. But would you believe it? This was the only bicycle to be found in the entire village. We could have ordered a Comet, of course, but then it never would have arrived in time for your birthday. Once you had seen this one, we were sure you wouldn't mind."

Jean-Pierre managed a weak little smile and shook his head several times to show Maman and Papa that he didn't mind. How could they know how important it was to him? But from that day on, the entire world seemed so dark and gloomy, Jean-Pierre had the hopeless feeling that nothing would ever make it right again.

Seeing Claude was now out of the question, and Jean-Pierre vowed to stop seeing him for the rest of the summer. He took to riding his bicycle later in the day when he knew that Claude would have gone home. And as for Georges and Albert, they teased him harder than ever since he had expressed his wish to become a *sous-sous chef*.

Papa's kitchen, which he had loved so much, now filled him with misery. And whenever he was standing in his corner watching, he felt as though he should be wearing a dunce cap.

"Ah, good day, little *Sous-Sous*," Georges might cry, bowing as low as his fat stomach would permit. "And how is our great *sous-sous chef* this fine morning? May we take the liberty of welcoming our famous new *sous-sous chef* to our humble kitchen?"

"Sh!" commanded Albert, holding up his toothpick of a finger. "Our great *sous-sous chef* is looking. He is listening. He is learning. Let us not disturb this important process. Let us not waste his many talents."

"One begins to wonder about these many talents, however," added Georges thoughtfully. "I have never seen them displayed, have you?"

"Truthfully, no," replied Albert. "But then what can you expect when even our father says he is not ready to peel so much as a potato in just the right way?"

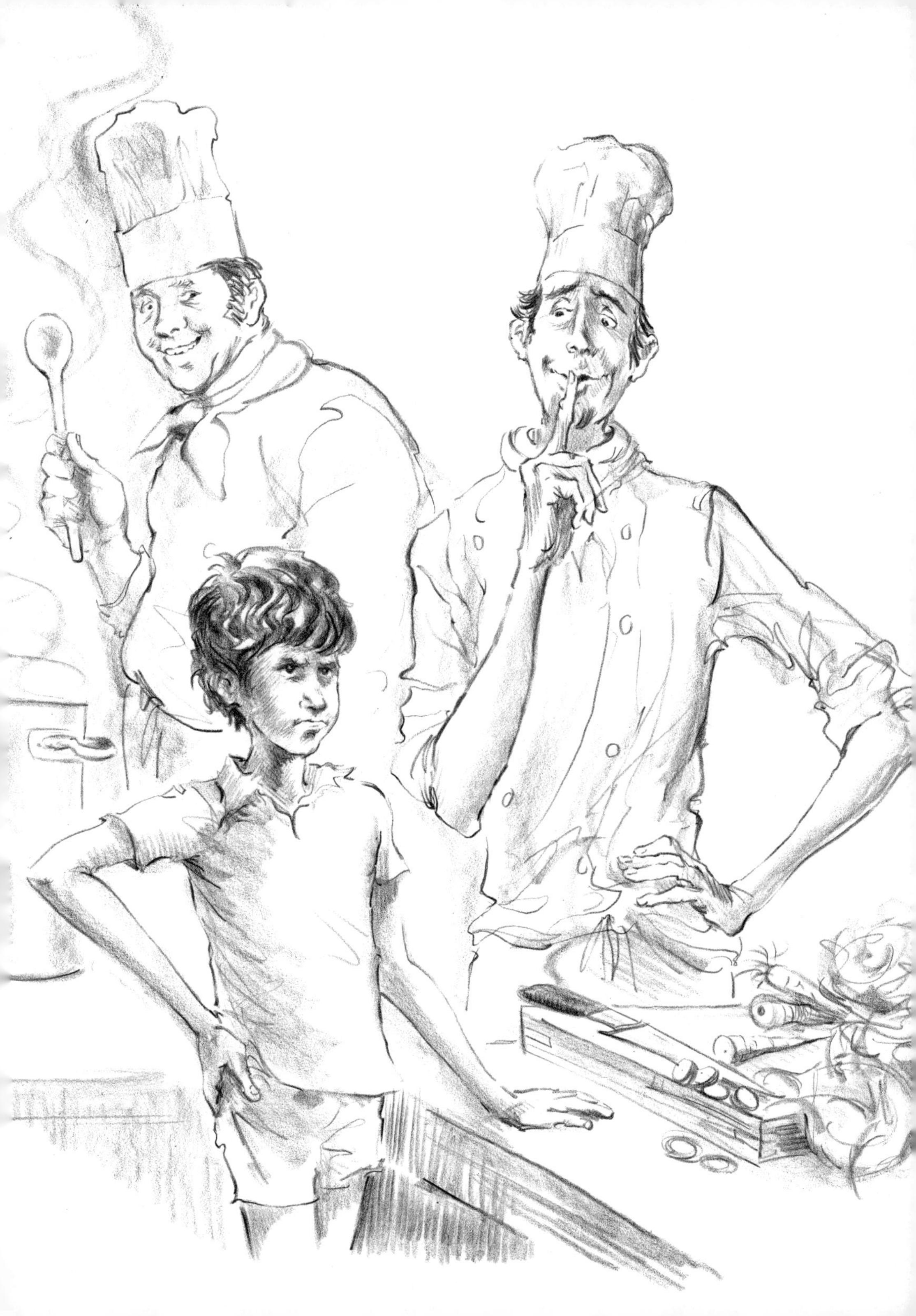

The result of their teasing was that with each passing day Jean-Pierre grew more unhappy, and more angry. One night he had a dream. In it Papa, Georges, and Albert had surrounded him in his kitchen corner, all pointing at him and laughing. "You couldn't peel so much as a potato in just the right way," they chanted again and again. "You couldn't peel so much as a potato in just the right way!"

All of Jean-Pierre's held-in rage and disappointment and despair came out in one big burst. "Is that so?" he shouted aloud in his dream so furiously that he woke himself up. "We'll see about that!" He knew that he had been dreaming, and yet the dream was so real that he found himself pulling on his clothes in the dark.

Silent as a thief he crept downstairs. The dark empty kitchen seemed strange and unfriendly at this hour. And yet he knew that soon the cheerful kitchen noises would begin. He had no time to waste. Quickly and quietly he set to work.

Each day either Georges or Albert peeled

enough potatoes for Papa's soups and stews and other dishes to fill the great yellow bowl that Papa always kept beside him on a table next to the stove.

From the vegetable bin Jean-Pierre selected the firmest, finest potatoes he could find. Next, from the knife rack, he chose the paring knife with the sharpest blade. This was extremely important, for Papa hated waste of any kind. He liked the potato parings so thin you could almost see through them. And the eyes of the potatoes must be cut out so carefully that not a scrap of potato was lost.

At last he could begin! Slowly, steadily, the pile of potatoes grew. Jean-Pierre examined the parings. Thin as paper. He peered at the holes where the eyes had been. Small as pinpoints. Surely no one could do better, Jean-Pierre told himself happily. Not even Papa.

But when the yellow bowl was only half full, two frightening things began to happen. It started to grow light outside, which meant that Papa and Georges and Albert would be arriving shortly.

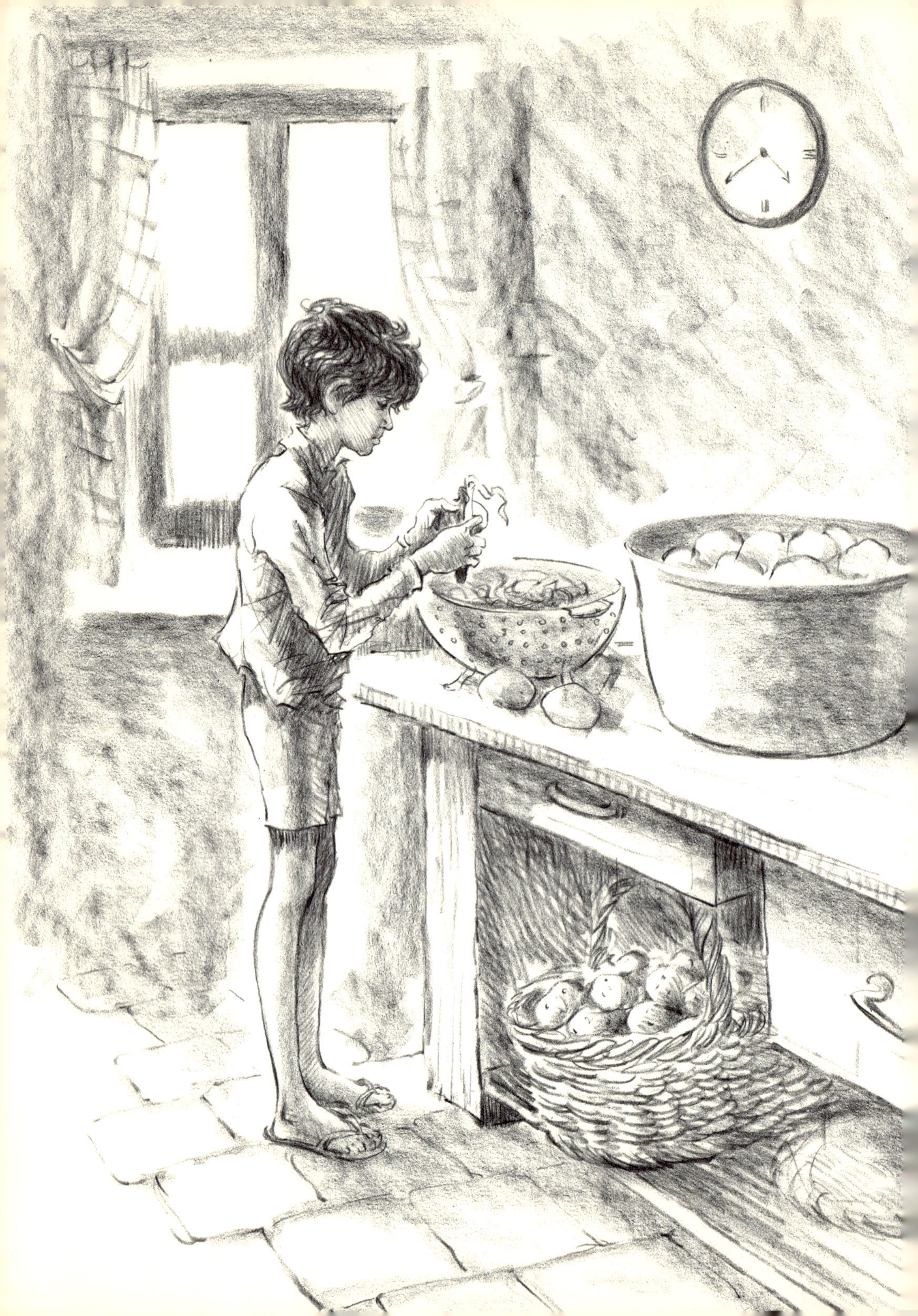

And worse, Jean-Pierre was growing so sleepy that he had to fight to keep his eyelids from falling like shutters over his eyes.

His back ached. His arms ached. His neck and shoulders ached. Peeling potatoes in "just the right way" was much harder than Jean-Pierre had ever imagined. Still, he refused to give up. The sun was shining through the kitchen windows as Jean-Pierre finished the last potato.

With his final ounce of strength, he threw the potato peels into the pail under the sink, scrubbed the table clean, and stumbled to his corner, where he fell fast asleep on the floor.

He was awakened by the sound of the kitchen door banging open, and the loud voices of Georges and Albert. He sat up, rubbing his eyes, and slowly got to his feet.

"Well, look who's here!" cried Georges. "Now it's got so that our *sous-sous chef* even sleeps in the kitchen. Were you sleeping on the floor all night?"

"No," replied Jean-Pierre truthfully. He decided to say nothing more. He was determined that Papa should be the first to see the potatoes. For once, instead of his brothers' scorn, he wanted Papa's praise.

"Why don't you give up and act your age?" asked Albert. "Children like you need their rest. I wonder what Papa would say if he saw you lying on the floor like that? I've a good mind to tell him."

"Go ahead, tell him," said Jean-Pierre, sounding far calmer than he felt. As they began their early morning chores, neither Georges nor Albert was ever very far from the yellow bowl, and with each passing moment the risk grew.

Georges, looking for a special pan, peered into Papa's stove, not three inches from where the peeled potatoes sat. Albert dropped a spoon which landed directly in front of the table. At last, when Jean-Pierre was beginning to feel that he couldn't bear to wait another minute, Papa pushed through the swinging door.

"Good morning, good morning," shouted Papa, making his usual beeline for the stove. "What early birds we have here this morning!"

"You have no idea *how* early," said Albert gleefully. "Why, Jean-Pierre even—"

But Albert got no further. Papa's mind was already on his cooking. "Fine, fine," he said absentmindedly. "It's the early bird that catches the worm, I always say. Now, with the luncheon menu that I have planned, I shall need diced carrots, onions, mushrooms, celery. Georges? Albert?"

Georges reached for the great bunch of celery lying close by, and took from the knife rack his chopping knife. "All done, Papa," he said. "Except the celery, and I can do that right now."

"Good," said Papa. "*Tiens, tiens,* I almost forgot. I was planning to make a hot potato soup with leeks, so are the potatoes—? Ah, yes," he continued, glancing into the yellow bowl. "I see that the potatoes are already peeled. Splendid. Now I can begin to—

"Just a minute!" he suddenly roared, examining the potatoes more closely. "Who peeled these, I should like to know? You, Georges? You, Albert?"

"Why, no, Papa," said Georges in astonishment.

"Very well, then, it was you, Albert," said Papa.

"No, Papa, not I," replied Albert.

"What do you take me for, a fool?" bellowed Papa, his face as dark as midnight. "There are the potatoes in the bowl. One of you is responsible, and I demand to know who."

Gazing into the yellow bowl which Papa held pressed against his stomach, Georges looked at Albert. Albert looked at Georges. Papa stood glowering at them both, waiting for an answer, while Jean-Pierre wished that he were miles away riding his bicycle.

"I am waiting," said Papa in his quiet voice which was far more frightening than when he shouted. "Which of you peeled these potatoes?"

As though a light switch had been turned on in their heads at one and the same time, Georges and Albert cried together: "Jean-Pierre!"

"What?" gasped Papa. "Why, how can that be? Surely if this were so, one of you would have noticed it."

"How could we have noticed?" asked Albert. "Jean-Pierre must have peeled them during the night. We found him asleep on the floor when we got here."

Papa shook his head from side to side as though he couldn't believe what he had heard. "Is this true, Jean-Pierre?" he asked.

By now, Jean-Pierre was so scared that he only wanted to run and hide in some secret place where

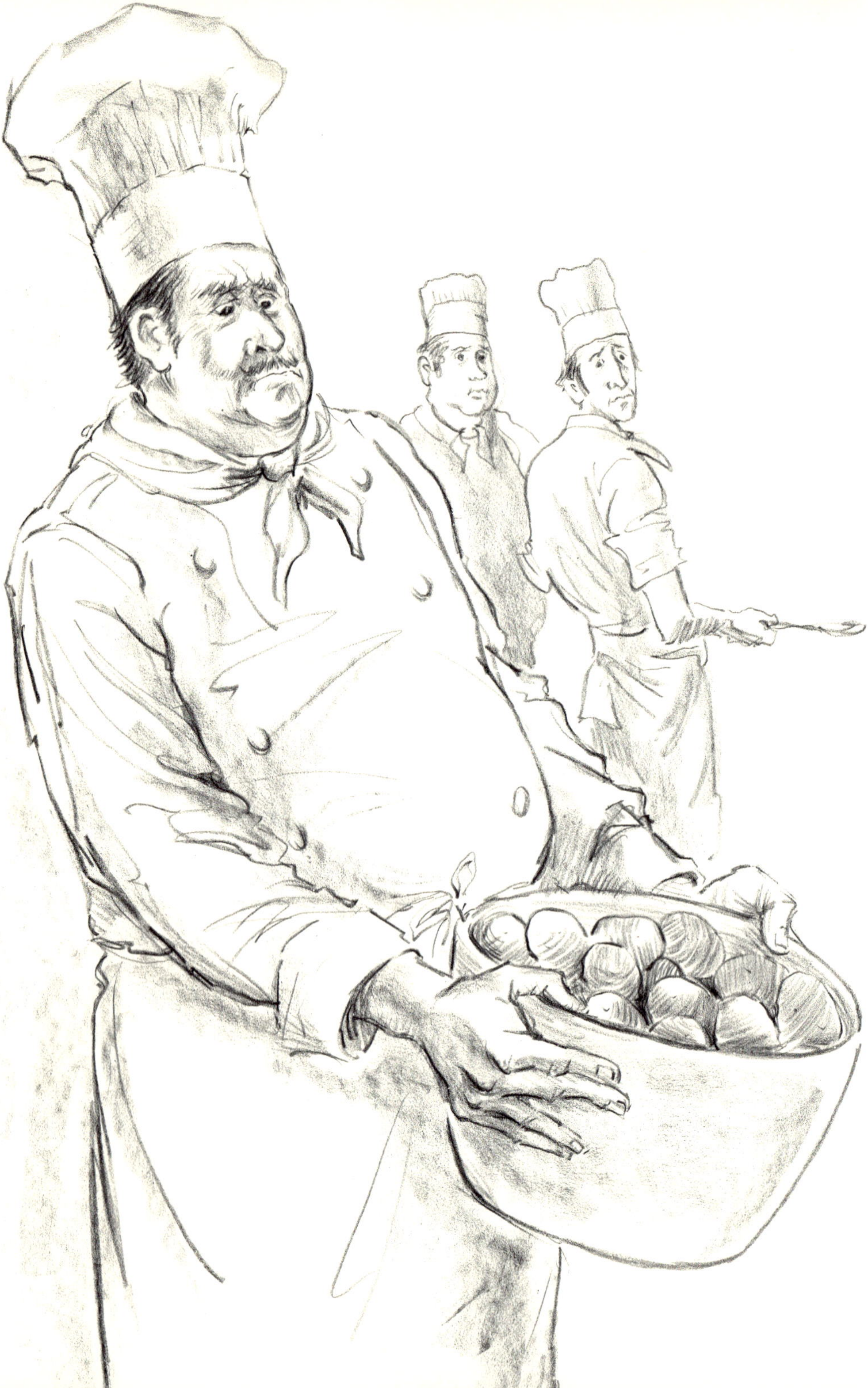

he couldn't be found. In answer to Papa's question he merely nodded his head, waiting, and dreading to hear how he had failed.

"I see," said Papa in the same frighteningly quiet voice he had used with Georges and Albert. "Well, this is very serious. Very serious indeed. You know perfectly well that in his own kitchen the chef makes the rules and gives the instructions. You have disobeyed mine. What were they? Do you even remember?"

"Yes, Papa, I remember," whispered Jean-Pierre.

"And yet, in spite of that, you chose to forget," said Papa. "What did I tell you?"

"You said that it would take me many more years of looking and listening and learning before I could do a simple task like peeling a potato in just the right way," said Jean-Pierre unhappily.

"Exactly," said Papa. "And now at last, perhaps you will have some respect for what I say. These potatoes are ruined, and will have to be thrown out. Rather than use potatoes like these I would close my restaurant."

Papa, still holding the bowl, walked over to Jean-Pierre. "Look at them!" he commanded.

In one sickening glance Jean-Pierre saw that the potatoes had turned a muddy brown. At once he knew what he had neglected to do, what he had seen his brothers do a hundred times.

"Yes," continued Papa, examining the potatoes carefully. "I can see that the peelings are as thin as they should be. The eyes are small and well pared.

So far so good. Unfortunately, however, you made one enormous mistake. You forgot to cover them in cold water. Surely you must know that once a potato has been peeled, if it stands without being placed in cold water, it turns dark in color."

With one angry gesture Papa emptied the entire bowlful of potatoes into the same pail where Jean-Pierre had thrown the peelings.

"And so you see, Jean-Pierre," said Papa, "in order to rise to the top, one must be willing to start at the bottom. There is no other way." Papa turned to his stove. The subject was ended, and Jean-Pierre's nightmare had come true. He wasn't ready even to peel potatoes in just the right way.

The very next night Jean-Pierre was wakened by moaning and groaning, and there was the sound of heavy footsteps pacing to and fro. Jean-Pierre tried telling himself that he was having another nightmare. But even as he told himself this, he knew that the noise was real. Someone was in deep trouble. Papa!

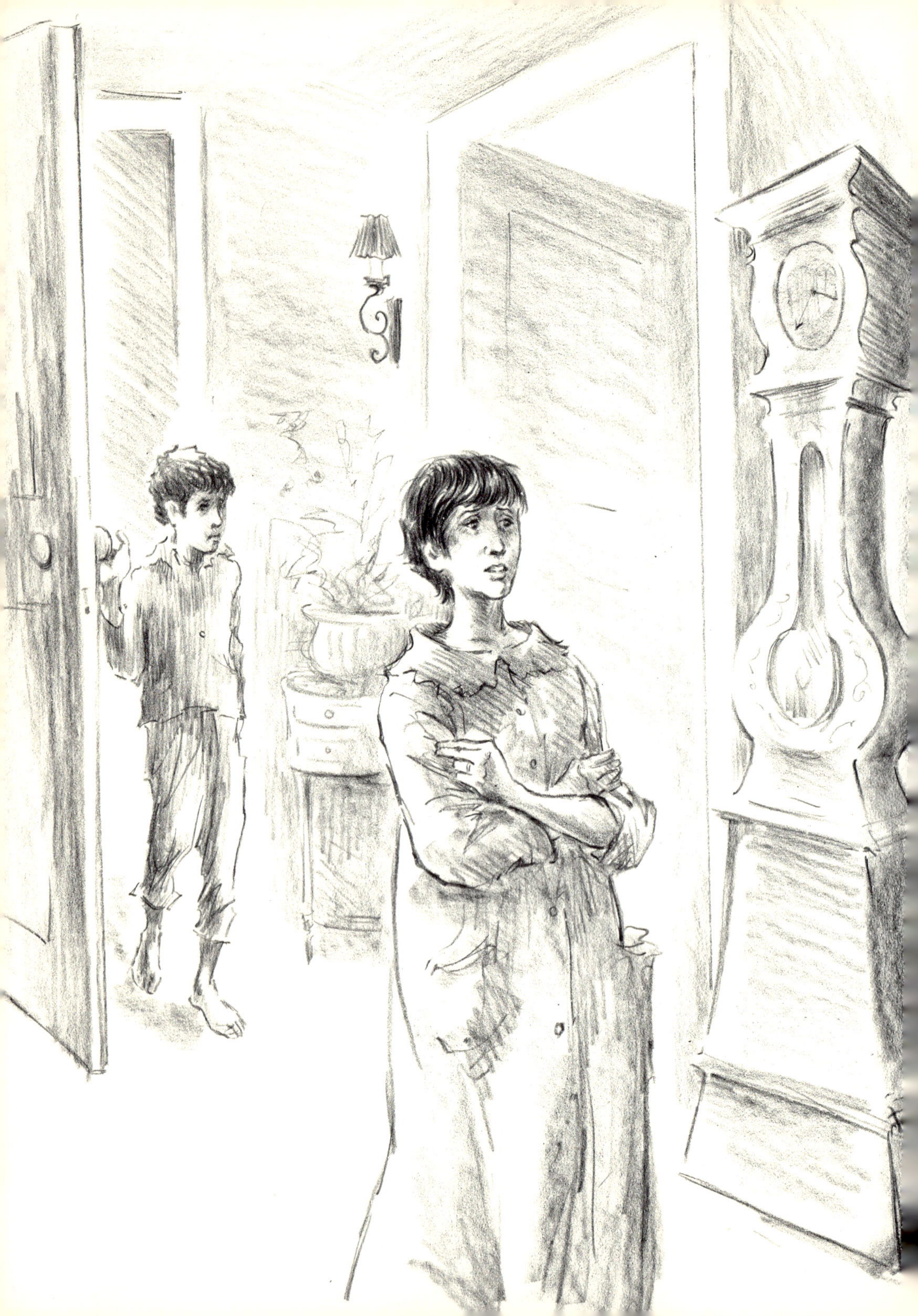

Half asleep and shaking with fear, Jean-Pierre opened the door of his room and stumbled into the hall. Papa, his left jaw swollen to the size of a baseball, was pacing up and down with Maman right behind him, making suggestions.

"There is nothing better than oil of cloves for a toothache, Henri," she was saying. "Let me get it for you. Or an ice pack to dull the pain. Or both.

Yes, both would be best, I think. At least they will give you some relief until you can go to the dentist tomorrow."

Maman caught sight of Jean-Pierre. "Your father has been up with a violent toothache most of the night," she explained, "and as usual he won't listen to a word I say. Henri! Will you kindly stop that dreadful noise and do as I tell you for once?" she shouted in a sudden rage.

But Papa only moaned and groaned the harder, rolling his eyes toward the ceiling, smiting himself on the forehead, and crying out "Dirty Pig!" and "Stupid Camel!" for all the world as though he had just made a *Chocolat Chardin* that failed.

"Well, I give up!" cried Maman. "If you won't let me help you, there's absolutely no use in my staying here."

For the first time Papa seemed to hear what Maman was saying. "Have you forgotten about tomorrow?" he yelled. "How can I possibly go to the dentist with all that I have to do? Why, I could have fifty toothaches, ten times worse than this one, and still not be able to leave to go to the dentist."

"Ha!" exclaimed Maman triumphantly. "It is *you* who have forgotten about tomorrow. Tomorrow is Monday, and since the restaurant is always closed on Mondays, you will have all day to go to the dentist."

"Have you taken leave of your senses?" asked Papa. "You don't remember the telephone call I received from His Honor, the Mayor? You don't remember that he asked me as a special favor to open the restaurant for him tomorrow?"

"Ah, *mon Dieu*," cried Maman. "Forgive me, Henri. I *had* forgotten!"

Jean-Pierre didn't understand. "But why should the Mayor want Papa to open the restaurant tomorrow?" he wanted to know.

"You may well ask," Maman replied mournfully. "Monsieur Guillaume Gervais, the famous writer of the guidebook *Where to Dine in France*, is on a tour of this part of the country. He has only one day here, and he especially wanted to have lunch at Papa's restaurant, having heard so much about it. When he discovered that we were closed tomorrow he called the Mayor, expressing his disappointment. The Mayor assured him that he would take care of it, and would even join him here for such a great occasion.

"Need I tell you how important this is? Hundreds of tourists all over Europe, all over America, for that matter, read Monsieur Gervais' guidebook. If he writes that he likes Papa's cooking, the tourists will flock here all next summer. If he doesn't, they will flock somewhere else. And with such a toothache, how can Papa ever manage to—"

Maman broke off and began wringing her hands. The possibility of such a failure was too dreadful to bear thinking about. Jean-Pierre shifted from foot to foot and wished that there were something he could do to help. At the same time he longed to be back in bed.

Meanwhile Papa had left off moaning and groaning and was gazing thoughtfully at the ceiling. When at last he spoke, it was clear that he had reached a decision.

"When an actor has a toothache, does he refuse to act?" shouted Papa, his face turning scarlet at the very idea of such an outrage. "When a doctor has a toothache, does he refuse to see a sick patient? And when a chef such as I is asked to cook a special luncheon for so important a guest, do I apologize and run off to the dentist like a weakling?"

Papa paused, and glared at Maman as though daring her to disagree with him. "No," he went on. "I would never forgive myself. I would be a disgrace to my profession. The Mayor has asked me to choose and prepare the menu. Very well. I intend to cook such a luncheon as he and this Monsieur Gervais have never tasted before, toothache or no toothache."

"Ah, *mon cher* Henri," said Maman lovingly. "How truly wonderful you are. I might have known. Now I shall fetch the oil of cloves and the ice pack, and perhaps you will sleep a little. You need all the rest you can get before your long, hard day begins."

Maman and Papa returned to their room, and Jean-Pierre went back to bed. But tired as he was, he couldn't sleep. Tossing and turning, he asked himself over and over how poor Papa, with his terrible toothache, could possibly cook his great luncheon.

And yet everything was going as smoothly as always by the time Jean-Pierre took up his usual place in the kitchen corner. Georges and Albert were hard at work. And although Papa's jaw was even more swollen than it had been the night before, he was as busy at his stove as though nothing had happened.

In fact, Jean-Pierre noticed only one thing out of the ordinary. Instead of the one or two cups of his strong, black coffee that he usually drank to quiet his nerves, Papa had no sooner finished one cup than he started on another. A bad sign! And yet, when he had drunk a third, and then a fourth cupful, Papa began mumbling aloud to himself what to do. A good sign!

"So," began Papa. "Clearly this Monsieur Gervais has been to all of the most elegant, the most luxurious restaurants in France. His wanting to come here means that he is also interested in fine cooking in a simple country setting such as this.

"Very well, then, that is exactly what he shall have. Nothing too fancy. Nothing too elaborate. But each dish must be perfect—perfect!"

Humming a song that had no tune, Papa went to the refrigerator and gently poked with his finger his *Oeufs à la Gelée*. "Jellied eggs—a fine beginning for the luncheon: light, simple, refreshing," he proclaimed. "And the fish? Next, let us examine my *Turbot*."

Papa returned to his stove and lifted the lid of a huge saucepan where the turbot was slowly poaching in white wine. "Ah," he cried, kissing his fingers in the air. "*Magnifique!*"

He opened the oven door, sniffed deeply several times, and basted the roast he was cooking. "Juicy, rare, tender. What, I ask you, is better than a noble *Filet de Boeuf?*" Since Papa was really asking no one but himself, nobody answered.

"And now," said Papa, contentedly rubbing his hands together, "now for my *Chocolat Chardin,* the *pièce de résistance* of the meal—any meal."

Jean-Pierre, who had been breathlessly watching Papa's every move, marveled at the way Papa seemed able to forget his pain, carried off as usual into his wonderful world of cooking. At last, Jean-Pierre's greatest moment in Papa's kitchen had arrived! Papa was ready to make his *Chocolat.*

It was at this point, to Jean-Pierre's horror, that Papa gave a loud groan. He wiped his perspiring forehead with the towel that he kept tucked into his apron, staggered over to the kitchen table, and slumped down, holding his head in his hands.

"Papa, what is it?" cried Georges in alarm. "Some aspirin? Should we call Maman?"

"No, no," Papa sighed wearily. "I just felt faint for a moment. My tooth is throbbing as though it were being pounded with a sledgehammer."

"Some coffee, then, to calm your nerves?" asked Albert.

"Thanks, yes," said Papa gratefully, "for believe

me, my nerves have never been less calm." Papa drank the cupful in three large gulps, slowly got up from the table, and dragged himself to his stove. As Papa reached for the small saucepan that he always used when he began his *Chocolat,* Jean-Pierre's relief was so great that he found himself shaking as though he had taken a sudden chill.

"Now," began Papa in an almost inaudible voice, "first, we melt the chocolate v-e-r-y slowly..."

Jean-Pierre knew the familiar instructions that Papa always gave himself so well by now that he could have said them in his sleep. He gave a great yawn. He had been up much of last night. He had been up most of the night before.

Now he found his eyelids closing, closing against his will, just as they had in the middle of his potato peeling. He was so tired that for the first time he could remember he had no fear, no feelings of any kind, as the moment came for Papa to make "The Test." With his eyes still closed, he waited for Papa's joyous shout of *"Voilà!* Perfect! The best I've ever made!" But there was only silence.

How could this be? Jean-Pierre asked himself. He was used to Papa's exclamations of joy when his *Chocolat* had succeeded, and to his cries of rage when it failed. But silence? Never! He forced himself to open his eyes. Papa, looking almost as white as his cap and apron, was quietly closing the oven door!

One of two things had happened, Jean-Pierre quickly decided. Either he had dozed off while Papa was making "The Test," or Papa had forgotten to make it. In any case, shouldn't he warn Papa before it was too late?

"Papa!" he cried.

"I can't talk to you now, Jean-Pierre," said Papa, glancing at the kitchen clock. "I have to leave for the dentist. Please find Maman and ask her to come in."

"But, Papa," implored Jean-Pierre. "I don't know whether you—"

"Did you hear what I said?" shouted Papa. "Get Maman at once, and stop bothering me at a time like this."

Jean-Pierre went to get Maman, who was in the restaurant nervously straightening the silverware and glasses on the one table that would be occupied that day.

Hurrying into the kitchen, they found Papa taking off his chef's hat and beginning to untie his apron. "Well, *Chérie*," he said to Maman, "I leave everything in your capable hands.

"Albert, is the salad made? Good. And about the tiny peas—don't put them in until our guests arrive or they will be overdone. As for you, Georges, it is now one o'clock. My *Chocolat* must come out of the oven by one-thirty. No sooner. No later. Understood? *Très bien*."

"And now I must leave." Slowly Papa walked to the door, his shoulders bowed, his head down, the very picture of sorrow.

Maman began to cry. "Oh, Henri," she sobbed, running to embrace him. "All the pain and suffering you've endured. Such courage, such strength, such—"

Papa put his arms around her and gently patted

her on the back. "There, there," he rumbled soothingly. "There, there. All I ask is that you and Georges and Albert carry on as though nothing has happened so that our guests will feel relaxed and happy. Now, dry your eyes and let me see your charming smile."

Maman dabbed at her eyes with her dainty white apron and managed a weak little smile.

"Good! Excellent!" Papa exclaimed, beaming at her proudly. "Now I can go to the dentist with a light heart, and believe me, that is something that I rarely do!"

No more than two minutes after Papa had left, the Mayor and Monsieur Gervais arrived. Maman, who had been waiting near the door, hurried forward to greet them.

"Psst! Jean-Pierre," Georges called softly. "Go see what's happening."

Jean-Pierre ran to the door and opened it just enough to see and hear without being discovered. "Maman is welcoming them," he reported to Georges and Albert. "The Mayor is kissing her hand. Now he is introducing her to Monsieur Gervais. Monsieur Gervais is bowing, very polite, very correct."

"What's he look like?" Albert wanted to know.

"Tall, handsome, almost like a movie star," said Jean-Pierre excitedly. "And you should see his clothes! They look better than the ones we wear to weddings."

"What else?" demanded Georges.

"Monsieur Gervais is looking all around the restaurant at the photographs on the walls that people have signed and sent to Papa. He appears most impressed. He has just told Maman: " 'Madame, I can see that many famous people have dined at your restaurant, including His Honor, the Mayor, here.' "

"What did she say to that?" asked Albert.

"Exactly what you'd expect her to say," said Jean-Pierre in a superior tone. " 'Ah, but no one more famous than yourself, Monsieur.' "

"Good for her," chuckled Georges. "She knows what side her bread's buttered on!"

At this point, Jean-Pierre quickly let the door swing shut and scuttled back to his corner. "Here she comes!" he hissed.

"So far so good," said Maman as she entered the kitchen. "Already Monsieur Gervais has given me enough compliments to last a lifetime. Now let us see what he thinks of Papa's cooking. That is what he came for, after all."

Maman gave a quick glance around the kitchen. Everything seemed to be going as smoothly as Papa would have wished. Her first tray was ready and waiting for her, filled with bread, warm from the oven, and a silver dish of ice-cold pats of butter. She gave a satisfied nod, and disappeared with it through the swinging door.

It was at this very moment that a smell of burning began to fill the kitchen, and a thin trickle of black smoke came curling out of the oven.

Georges whirled around, his face as white as paper. Albert, who was at the stove cooking the tiny peas, reached for a pot holder, opened the oven door, and, without a word, brought out Papa's *Chocolat*—burned to a crisp!

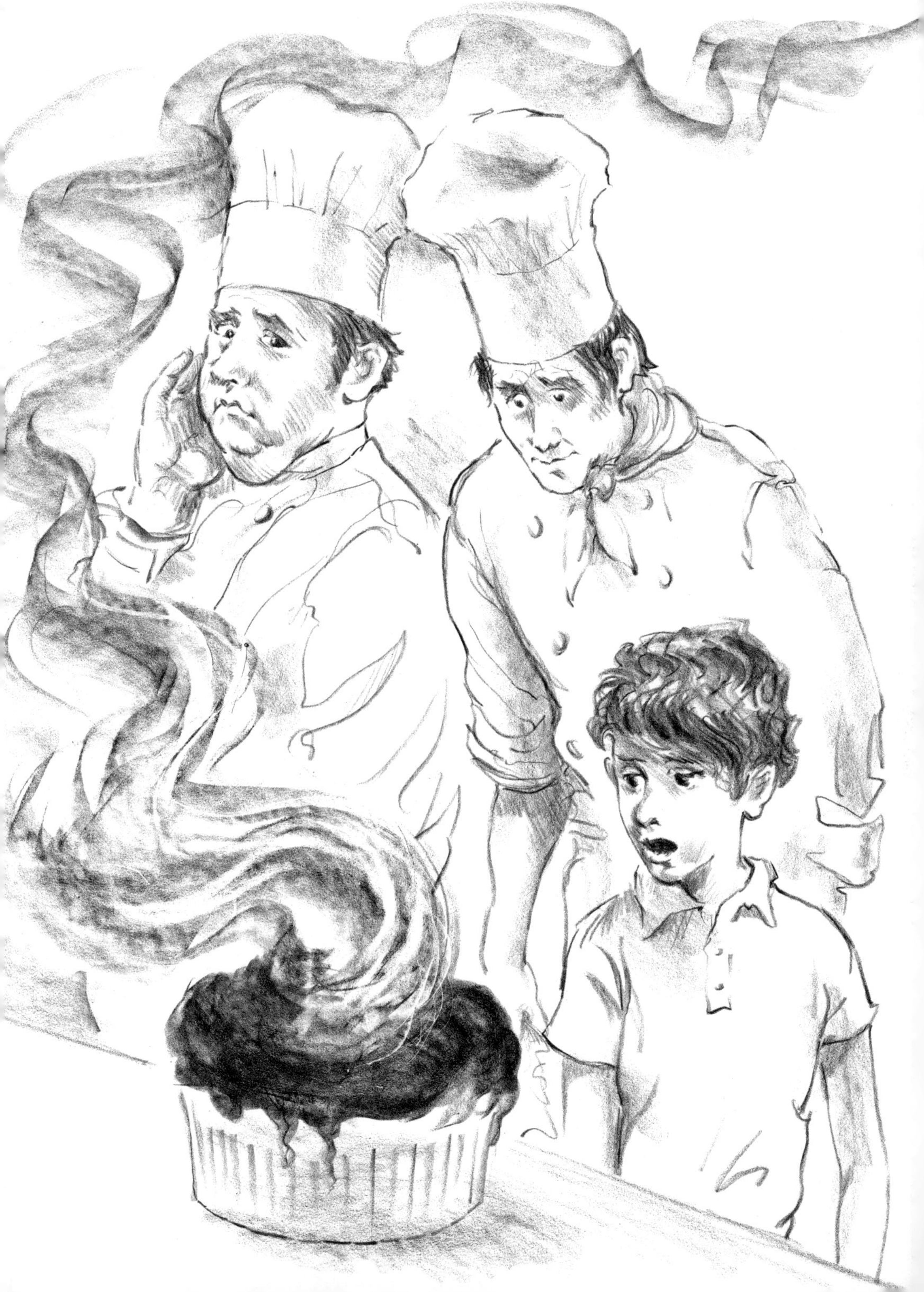

Like statues the three brothers stood staring at the ruined *Chocolat*. Jean-Pierre began to feel dizzy and sick. Just as he had feared, Papa had not made "The Test" after all, and something had gone terribly wrong.

Maman came bustling in. She put down her empty tray. She lifted her head and sniffed the air, her eyes wide with alarm. Then she saw Papa's ruined *Chocolat*. She had only one question to ask: "How did it happen?"

When Georges and Albert remained silent, she flew into one of her rages. "Speak up, you idiots," she cried. "What did you do? You left it in the oven too long, that's what!"

Georges shook his head sadly. "No, Maman, we did not keep it in the oven too long. Papa put the *Chocolat* in the oven at one o'clock. We were to leave it in for thirty minutes, he said. No more. No less. See for yourself. It is only twenty-five minutes past one. The *Chocolat* had another five whole minutes to cook."

"Yes, I can see," Maman said in a dead, flat voice. "I can also see that this is one of the worst calamities that has even befallen our restaurant." Maman broke off, unable to go on. "Well," she said at last, bravely controlling her emotion, "calamity or no calamity, Papa wanted us to carry on, and that is what we must do now. Georges, Albert, decide between you who is to make another *Chocolat,* and let us hope for the best."

But Georges and Albert remained as still as though a spell had been cast upon them. Maman began impatiently tapping her foot. "Well?" she asked. "I'm waiting. Which of you will make it?"

Finally Georges spoke up. "But Maman," he said, sounding frightened. "I have not the least idea how to make the *Chocolat,* and I doubt whether Albert has either."

"What?" gasped Maman. "I find this hard to believe. In fact, I refuse to believe it. After all the years you've spent—"

"You've forgotten, Maman, that *Chocolat Char-*

din is Papa's secret," interrupted Albert. "He has told no one how it is made—not even Georges and me. As for watching or listening to him make it, we're always too busy on the other side of the kitchen."

"*Mon Dieu!*" cried Maman, raising her eyes to the ceiling. "Now what?"

Suddenly Jean-Pierre's dizziness vanished. "I think I can make Papa's *Chocolat*," he said quietly.

"*You* make Papa's *Chocolat!*" exclaimed Georges in outrage. "An infant like you make Papa's greatest dish? I never heard of anything more ridiculous."

"You're really getting above yourself, you know that?" put in Albert. "Have you forgotten about the potatoes?"

Maman had been nervously glancing at the clock. Now she looked at Jean-Pierre as though truly seeing him for the first time.

"I am certain I can do it, Maman," Jean-Pierre said earnestly. "Well, *almost* certain. Because I stand so close to the stove, I have seen Papa make hundreds of *Chocolats*. I have heard everything he tells himself to do."

"What went wrong this time, do you know?" asked Maman. "Because if you don't, how can you be so sure that your *Chocolat* won't turn out to be just as great a failure?"

"Because I will begin at the beginning and make it step by step the way Papa does," Jean-Pierre replied. "I think Papa must have left out something on account of his toothache." And he forgot to make "The Test," or he would have known what it was, Jean-Pierre told himself silently, for there wasn't time to go into that now.

Again Maman glanced anxiously at the clock. Then she nodded and gave Jean-Pierre an affectionate hug. "Make Papa's *Chocolat*—you have my blessing," she said.

"Thank you, Maman," Jean-Pierre replied. "I'll do my very best."

Quickly Jean-Pierre went to Papa's stove. Since he was going to make the *Chocolat* step by step, exactly the way Papa did, he would leave out nothing that Papa used or needed or kept around him while he worked.

And, like Papa, he would tell himself aloud what to do, for he suddenly realized that this wasn't simply an endearing habit of Papa's. It was Papa's way of making sure that he would turn out a perfect *Chocolat*. Then, to be doubly sure, Papa finally made "The Test."

First, because Papa was never without the pot of strong, black coffee that he kept simmering on the back of the stove, Jean-Pierre took off the lid and peered inside. The pot was empty. This was scarcely surprising, for in order to calm his nerves today, Papa must have drunk the whole potful.

"I'll need some coffee," Jean-Pierre told himself aloud. "Good and strong. This pot is empty."

"Did you hear that?" asked Albert, nudging Georges. "Who does he think he is?"

"It's perfectly simple," replied Georges. "Already he thinks he's Papa. Our Great Chef's nerves need calming."

Maman, who had picked up the second tray that Georges and Albert had prepared for her, put it down with a bang. "You've both admitted that you cannot make Papa's *Chocolat*," she said angrily. "Jean-Pierre thinks he can. So there is to be no more of this childish teasing from now on. This isn't just a contest, you know. The entire future of this restaurant may depend on it."

Without another word, Maman picked up her tray once more and marched into the restaurant. Georges and Albert, looking sheepish, quietly returned to their work, while Jean-Pierre made the coffee and began assembling the ingredients Papa used for his *Chocolat*. With a voice that trembled at first, but that grew stronger and stronger as he went along, Jean-Pierre started telling himself aloud what to do.

"First, we melt the chocolate v-e-r-y slowly," he began, copying Papa's every word, his every gesture. "Now we put into the mixing bowl the sugar. *Très bien!* Next, we . . ."

As he continued measuring and mixing and telling himself aloud what to do, Jean-Pierre felt—he hoped—that everything was going well. But when he was almost through, his voice began to tremble again. In another moment he would know whether he had succeeded or failed.

Meanwhile, Maman had returned to the kitchen. Without having to turn around, Jean-Pierre could feel her sharp eyes watching every move he made. So much depended on him. So very much, Jean-Pierre was close to panic.

Suddenly it occurred to him that he had often eaten Papa's *Chocolat* after it was done, but that he had never once made "The Test." He had no idea what made Papa finally approve or disapprove of each *Chocolat* he made. He still didn't know how Papa's *Chocolat* had failed this time. Why, then, as Maman had pointed out, should his succeed?

Still, for better or for worse, the time had come. Jean-Pierre took a deep breath. He dipped his little finger into the *Chocolat*, tasted it, and cocked his head to one side in Papa's familiar gesture.

It tasted good, and although he had no way of knowing whether or not it was as good as Papa's, he was so relieved to have got this far that he had everything he could do to keep from shouting Papa's joyous cry of *"Voilà!* Perfect! The best I've ever made!"

Yet, as he started to open the oven door, he hesitated. He had forgotten something, something important. He was certain of it, but what? He closed his eyes and tried to picture how Papa looked, what he did during that final moment before he put the *Chocolat* into the oven, but nothing came of it. He waited so long that Maman became alarmed.

"What's wrong, Jean-Pierre?" she cried anxiously. "Aren't you feeling well?"

"Want some coffee to calm your nerves?" asked Albert sarcastically. "You made a whole new potful, remember?"

That was it! At last Jean-Pierre *did* remember! How could he have forgotten? "Yes, thanks for reminding me," he said to Albert. "Coffee's exactly what I want."

He filled to the brim a large cupful of coffee. And then, with an air of complete assurance, he poured the entire cupful over the *Chocolat!*

"Are you mad?" cried Maman, rushing forward. "Do you want to ruin the entire thing? Papa makes his coffee to drink, to calm his nerves, not to pour over the *Chocolat*."

"He does both, Maman," answered Jean-Pierre, trying to sound far more certain than he felt. Had he really seen Papa do this, or was he merely imagining it? No, he told himself firmly. He was *not* imagining it.

"Papa always pours a cupful of coffee over the *Chocolat* just before it goes into the oven. Only today, you see, he drank it all up because of his toothache."

"Well," said Maman in a deeply depressed tone, "it's too late now in any case. The proof of the pudding is in the eating. We shall have to wait and see about this one."

Maman returned with her next tray to the restaurant. Georges and Albert went back to their work, shaking their heads. Alone and unnoticed, full of doubt and fear, Jean-Pierre opened the oven door and gently placed the *Chocolat* inside.

He looked at the clock to make sure that the *Chocolat* would cook for a half hour—no more, no less. And now, as Maman had said, the waiting time had begun. After the first fifteen minutes, Jean-Pierre felt more hopeful. He sniffed the air, but so far there was no smell of burning. He glanced at the oven door, but not a single trace of black smoke was escaping.

The time finally passed. The *Chocolat* had been cooking for exactly a half hour. Jean-Pierre took it out of the oven and placed it on the table next to the stove.

"How is it? Did it turn out all right?" Maman's voice seemed to come from a great distance behind him.

In a daze, Jean-Pierre turned around and looked across the kitchen. "I don't know how it is, Maman," he told her. "At least this time it didn't burn."

"Well . . . that's something," said Maman dubiously. "In fact, it's a great deal," she added quickly, looking with concern at Jean-Pierre's troubled face. "But no matter what, I am deeply grateful to you, Jean-Pierre, for without you there would be no *Chocolat* at all." To show that she meant what she said, Maman left the kitchen carrying Jean-Pierre's *Chocolat* as proudly as though it were Papa's own.

She was not so calm, however, when she returned. Now she allowed herself to express the fright she had been feeling all along as the luncheon drew to a close.

"Where is Papa?" she demanded, looking accusingly at Georges and Albert as though they had hidden him somewhere. "You know how he insists on greeting his guests at the end of the meal, and he was especially anxious to greet the Mayor and Monsieur Gervais."

"Maman, he sensible," pleaded Georges. "He will surely be back at any moment now. The dentist probably kept him waiting."

"Be sensible, you say," cried Maman, squeezing her arms tightly across her chest as though to keep herself from falling apart. "How am I to be sensible when I have to tell Papa that his greatest achievement, the one he has labored all his life to perfect, his *Chocolat Chardin,* has failed?"

"Don't tell him!" chorused Georges and Albert.

"The burned *Chocolat* has been thrown away, and I washed out the bowl and put it back on the shelf," added Georges. "So if you don't tell him, how is he to know?"

"Oh, he'll know," Maman said hopelessly. "Besides, it wouldn't be fair to Jean-Pierre, who has worked so hard. Papa would want to know, I'm sure, even if—"

Maman cut herself off before she said what Jean-Pierre knew she was thinking: "even if Jean-Pierre's *Chocolat* turns out to be another disaster."

As he listened to this conversation, Jean-Pierre's thoughts were turning around in his head like squirrels in a cage. He *did* want Papa to know. He had hoped that just this once Papa would be proud of him. For a fleeting moment he toyed with the idea of telling Papa himself. It was tempting, but he quickly put it aside. In his heart he knew that Georges and Albert were right. There was only one thing to say, and he said it.

"They are right, Maman. Don't tell Papa. If my *Chocolat* is good, he need never know. If it isn't, he's bound to find out anyway. So why tell him unless you have to? Why not wait and see what happens?"

Maman looked so relieved that Jean-Pierre felt sad and noble at the same time. "Oh, Jean-Pierre," she cried. "I know how hard this must be for you. Are you quite sure you don't mind?"

Jean-Pierre put as much indifference into his voice as he could. "Of course," he said carelessly.

"Well, all right," said Maman. "I'll do everything in my power to keep Papa from knowing."

"Keep Papa from knowing what?" boomed an unmistakable voice. There stood Papa in the doorway! They had all been so absorbed in their discussion that they hadn't heard a sound from outside.

Although Papa's jaw was just as swollen as it had been when he left, some of the color had returned to his face, and he looked more like his usual sturdy self.

"Why—why, Henri . . ." Maman began weakly. "I'm so glad to see you. How did it go with the dentist? Did he pull out your tooth?"

"Yes," said Papa brusquely. "There was nothing to it. He gave me some pills to take. Now, what am I supposed not to know?"

"I cannot imagine what you mean, Henri," Maman replied innocently. "As a matter of fact, you *should* know that so far the luncheon has been a complete success."

"I see," said Papa, narrowing his eyes. "And exactly what do you mean by 'so far,' may I ask?"

"Just what I say," answered Maman. "The Mayor and Monsieur Gervais are not quite finished. They are still having their dessert and coffee. But judging by the way they seemed to enjoy the rest of the meal, they clearly found it excellent."

"Ummm," said Papa, turning his back on Maman and idly toying with a large spoon. "Then what am I not supposed to know?" he bawled, whirling around so fiercely that Maman jumped with fright.

"I have already told you, Henri," insisted Maman. "There is absolutely nothing you should not—"

"Don't try my patience, woman," roared Papa. "Something went wrong. I have only to look at your face. Now, what was it? My *Oeufs à la Gelée*? My *Turbot*? My *Filet de Boeuf*?"

Poor Maman was so upset by now that she didn't trust herself to speak. Silently she shook her head to each of Papa's questions.

"Very well, then," said Papa, finally coming to the last, the worst, the most shattering possibility. "If it was none of these, it must be my *Chocolat*."

Sadly Maman lowered her eyes. "Since you insist, Henri, yes, it *was* your *Chocolat*," she said. "It started to burn five full minutes before it was time to take it from the oven. And don't blame Georges," she quickly added. "I happen to know that he never took his eyes from the clock."

"My *Chocolat* burn?" Papa gasped incredulously. "That is altogether impossible. How did it happen?"

"None of us knows, Henri," said Maman. "Not even Jean-Pierre here, who—"

"Jean-Pierre!" cried Papa. "And exactly where does *he* fit into the picture I should like to know?" Papa turned and glared at Jean-Pierre as though he were a total stranger who had somehow wandered into the kitchen by mistake.

Maman's whole manner changed. "Where does he fit into the picture?" she asked spiritedly. "Why, he made a second *Chocolat*, that's what. Only *his* didn't burn."

Papa seemed to find this beyond belief. "Do you mean to stand there and tell me that Jean-Pierre made my *Chocolat*?" Papa shouted. "No one but myself has ever made my *Chocolat!*"

"Well, now someone has," Maman declared. "And now if you want to greet your guests, you had better get ready. It is already after two o'clock."

Without so much as a backward glance, Maman swept into the restaurant. Papa stalked to the tiny closet where he kept his chef's hat, his jacket, and his apron.

Moments later Maman came bursting through the door with such force that the empty dishes rattled on her tray. "Henri, Jean-Pierre, listen to this!" she cried joyously. "The *Chocolat* has never been more admired. It was a huge success—a *succès fou*. Now, what do you think of that? Isn't it wonderful? Henri, are you ready? They are waiting for you."

"Yes," said Papa grimly. "I am ready." And staring straight ahead, he stormed out of the kitchen.

"Oh, Jean-Pierre," exclaimed Maman. "I am so proud of you! I admit that I had some doubts, but you have succeeded beyond my wildest dreams..."

On and on went Maman, while Jean-Pierre stood in his corner, hating Papa. Dressed in his snowy white chef's uniform, Papa was the grandest man on earth. Jean-Pierre had told himself this time after time. How much he had always loved

Papa, admired him, looked up to him. Well, now he didn't any more.

Papa was a tyrant, a mean, ungrateful tyrant. He yelled like a spoiled brat when things didn't go exactly his way, and he hadn't so much as a kind word for you when they did. Oh, you could work for him. You could kill yourself working for him, but what did he care? No, Jean-Pierre decided. He would never be a *sous-chef* in Papa's kitchen. In somebody else's, maybe, but not in Papa's.

Maman had been right from the start. Why should he spend so much time in Papa's kitchen? He would take her advice at last. He would get on his bicycle and ride as fast and as far as he could, and for all he knew he might never come back.

Jean-Pierre waited until Maman began helping Georges and Albert with the dishes. Then, while her back was turned, quickly, silently, he stole to the shed. He was wheeling out his bicycle when Papa, the very last person he expected to see, came running up, red-faced and out of breath.

"Why are you leaving? Where are you going?" asked Papa.

Startled as he was, Jean-Pierre noticed that Papa looked deeply concerned. "For a ride on my bicycle," he replied, while the tone of his voice said: "What business is it of yours?"

"Must you go now? This very minute?" asked Papa. "Could you not wait for a short while?"

"I could, but I don't want to," Jean-Pierre answered defiantly.

"Not even as a favor to me?" asked Papa.

Never before, in all his life, could Jean-Pierre remember Papa's speaking this way. Papa was asking a favor of him, Jean-Pierre!

Although he tried to stay angry, Jean-Pierre found himself saying, "All right, I'll wait. But why?"

"Never mind why," said Papa with the old, familiar note of authority that Jean-Pierre knew so well. "Just come with me. Oh, yes. Look in the tool chest, will you please? I need a screwdriver."

Jean-Pierre couldn't imagine why Papa needed

a screwdriver, but he found one and handed it to him.

"Thank you," said Papa. "Shall we go?"

But instead of stopping in the kitchen, as Jean-Pierre had expected, Papa kept right on going. Then, stretching out his hand, he led Jean-Pierre through the kitchen door into the restaurant, straight to the table where sat the Mayor and Monsieur Gervais!

"Well, well, Jean-Pierre," exclaimed the Mayor heartily. "We have been waiting for you. We wanted to congratulate you on that fine *Chocolat* you made today. If your father hadn't told us, I never would have known the difference. It was so good, in fact, that I thought he had surpassed himself—a difficult thing to do."

"Oh, you know how it is, Your Honor," said Papa modestly. "The younger generation learns from the old, who, after all, are no longer so bright and so quick."

"Nonsense, Monsieur Chardin," said the Mayor. "It will be many a long day before anyone, even

Jean-Pierre here, can improve on your cooking."

"I know of few chefs who could," added Monsieur Gervais. "Thank you, Monsieur Chardin, for a most memorable luncheon. You are carrying on in the best tradition of French cooking, where the sons learn from the fathers, who, in turn, have learned from *their* fathers."

Monsieur Gervais rose from the table and bowed first to Papa and then to the Mayor—and then, to Jean-Pierre's complete astonishment, to *him!* "And now I must be on my way," he said. "When my book is published I shall send both you, Monsieur Chardin, and you, Jean-Pierre, an autographed copy."

With another special bow to Papa, Monsieur Gervais left the restaurant. The Mayor, however, who was usually in such a hurry to get back to his many duties at City Hall, lingered on. It appeared that he had more to say.

"Jean-Pierre," he began, "I, too, have something to autograph for you. I asked your father's permission, and he gladly consented."

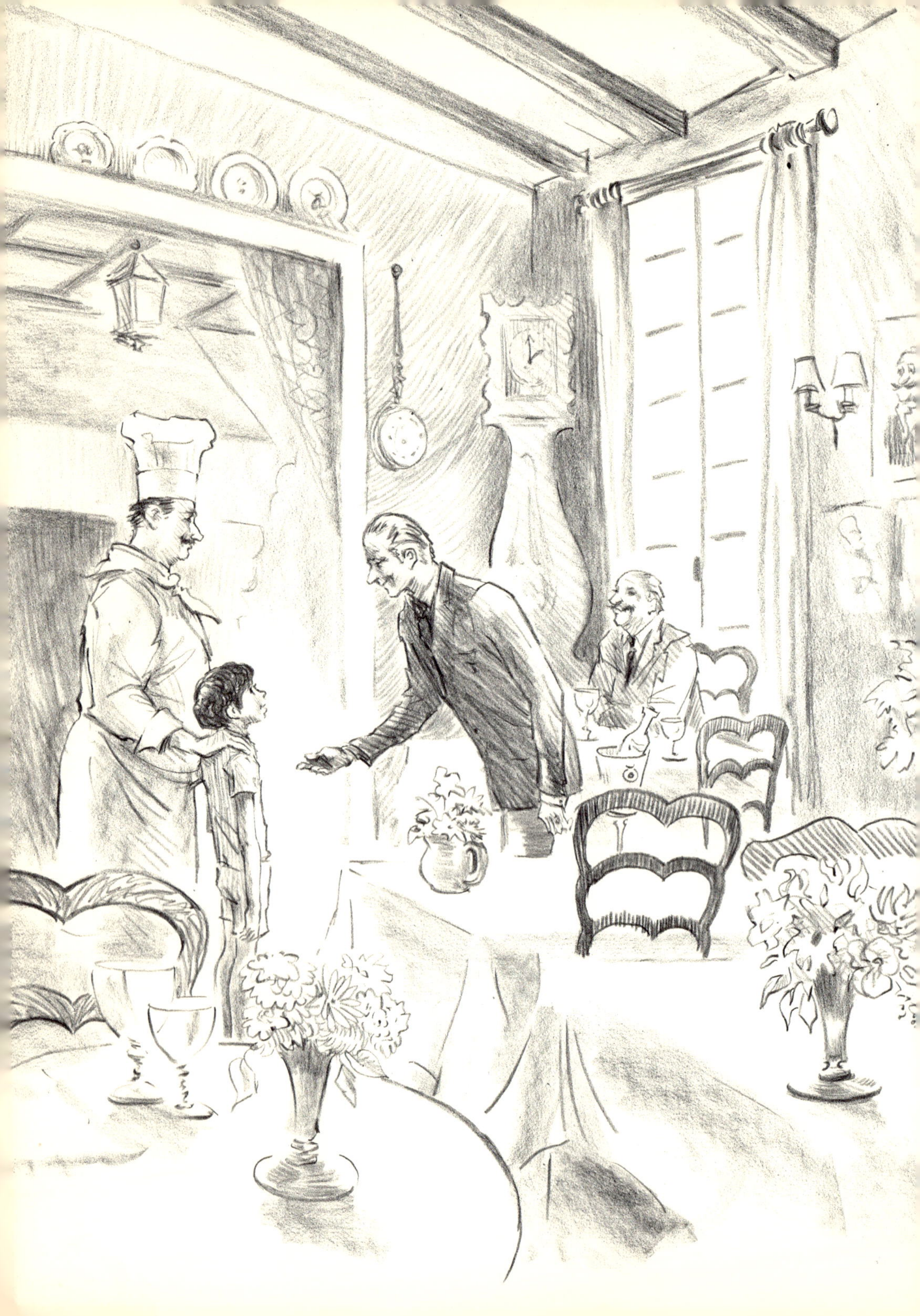

The Mayor reached under the table, and pulled out the giant photograph of himself that had hung on the restaurant wall for as long as Jean-Pierre could remember. He laid it on the table, and Papa, with the screwdriver Jean-Pierre had found for him, pried open the nails on the back. Then he lifted the photograph out of the frame and handed it to the Mayor.

The original autograph said: "To Monsieur Henri Chardin—a great chef," with the Mayor's signature underneath. Now, from an inside pocket, the Mayor pulled out a pen and added below in the same big, bold handwriting: "And to Jean-Pierre Chardin, who has shown that he has the makings of a great chef."

The Mayor put away his pen and looked at his watch. "Tck, tck, how did it ever get to be this late?" he asked. "Well, I must fly. Thank you again for everything, Monsieur Chardin. Take care of that painful-looking jaw of yours."

"Thank you, Your Honor, you have been most kind," murmured Papa.

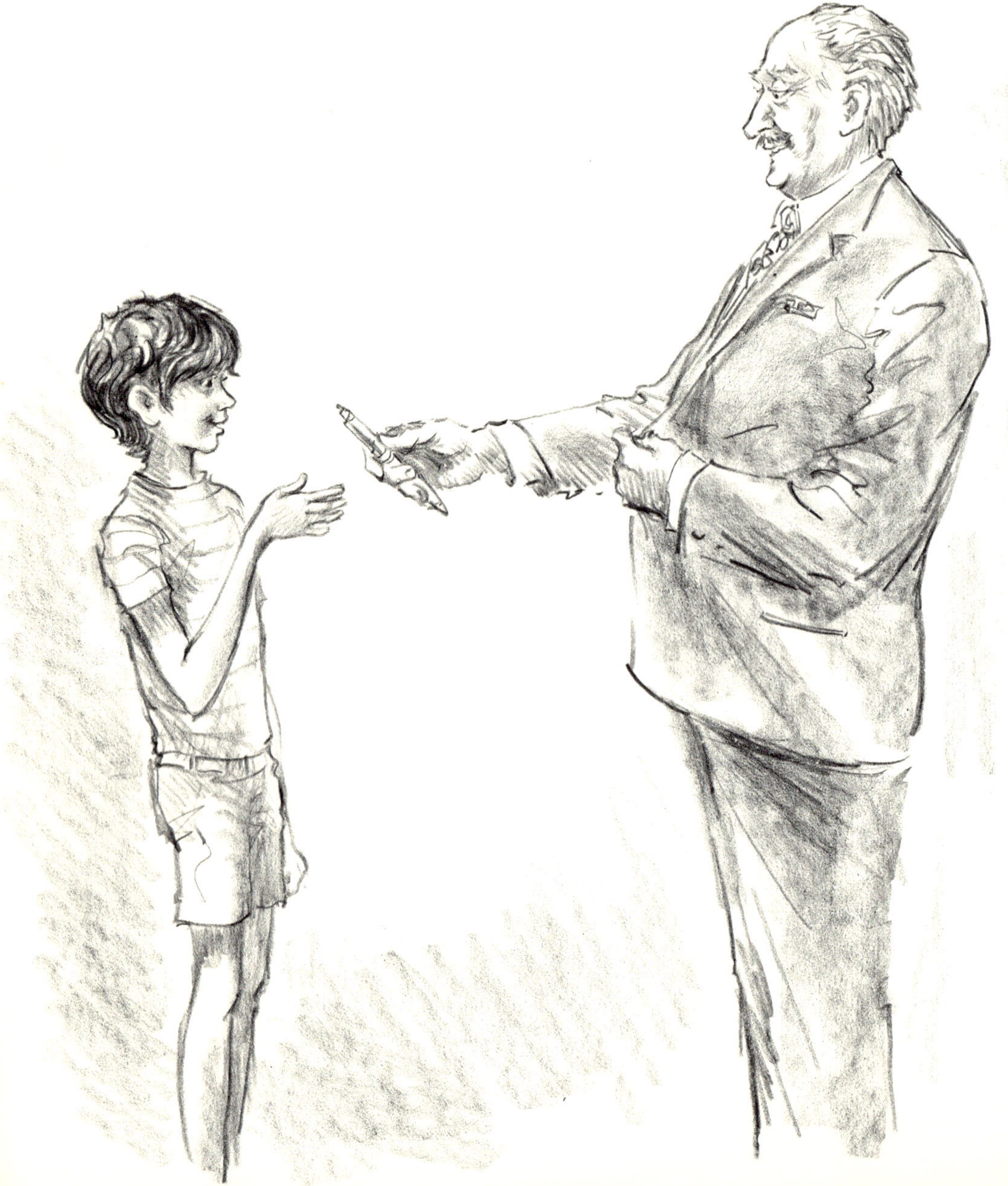

"Ah, no, it is *you* who have been kind," replied the Mayor. Just as Monsieur Gervais had done, the Mayor bowed first to Papa and then to Jean-Pierre. Then, just as he reached the door, the Mayor turned, took from his inside pocket the pen he had used, and handed it to Jean-Pierre.

"I want you to have this, Jean-Pierre, as a remembrance of your outstanding achievement today," he said. "Keep it as a reminder that when you cook your first meal, I wish to be your first guest."

The Mayor left so quickly that Jean-Pierre barely had time to stammer out an astonished "Thank you." With the Mayor gone, Papa returned the picture to the wall, reached for a glass of water, and gratefully swallowed two pills. Only then did he look at Jean-Pierre, who was staring in amazement at his beautiful gift.

"Yes, yes, very nice," said Papa, glancing at the pen. "But there are other things even more important than receiving a handsome present as a reward. Although I don't say you didn't earn it," he hastily added. "Sit down, Jean-Pierre. I think we need to have a talk. Why were you running away like that?"

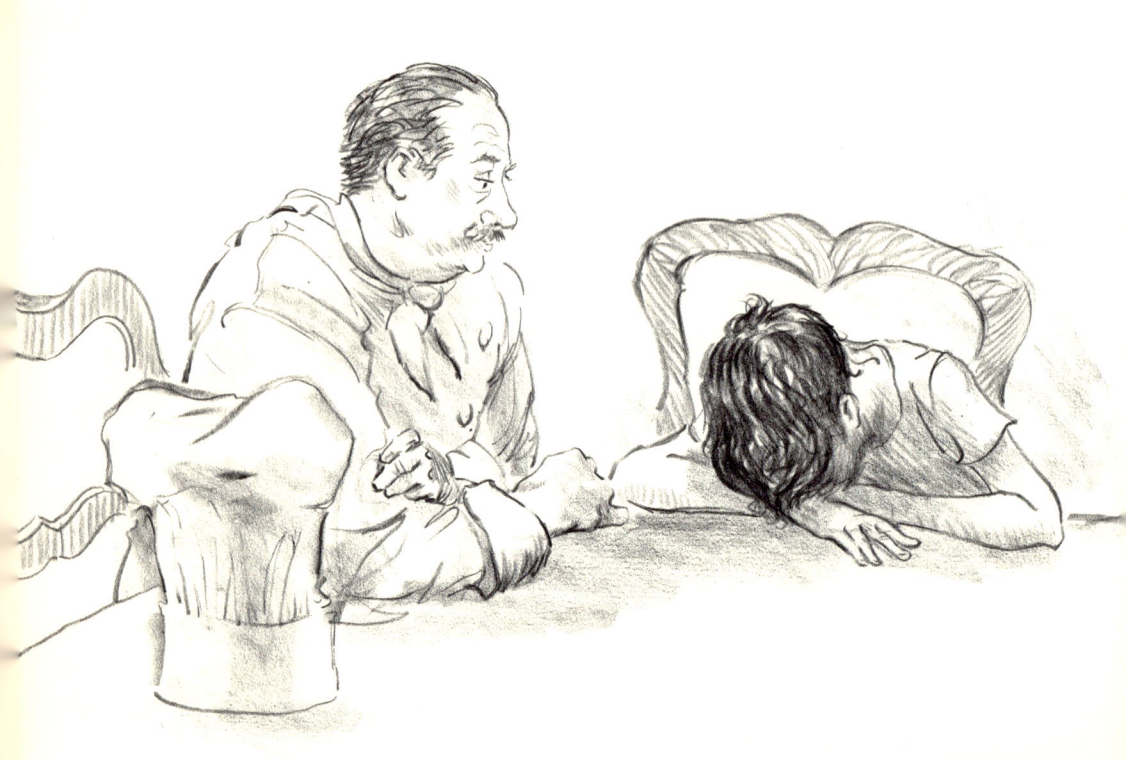

"Because—because," began Jean-Pierre. But he could go no further. From start to finish there had been too much of everything on this endless day. He put his head on the table and burst into tears. He wept and wept until he could weep no more. And when he had finally dried his eyes, a miraculous thing had happened. He was himself again, Jean-Pierre. And Papa was who he had always been. He was Papa! There was no longer any need for a talk, and both of them knew it.

Yet one question kept nagging at Jean-Pierre. Now, if ever, was the time to ask it, while Papa was in such an unusually mellow mood. "Papa," he began. "Why do you pour the coffee over your *Chocolat*?"

Papa looked mysterious. "Ah, that is my secret," he said. "But I shall tell you and you alone, Jean-Pierre, and then it will be *our* secret. Do I have your promise?"

Jean-Pierre nodded. "I promise," he said solemnly.

"Very well, then," commenced Papa. "There are three reasons for the coffee. First and most important, it keeps the *Chocolat* moist while it is cooking. Soon after Maman told me it had burned, I realized that only one thing could have happened. I had forgotten to pour in the coffee at the last minute as I always do. For all I know, I may have drunk the whole potful because of my toothache."

Jean-Pierre, who knew this to be the case, nodded in agreement.

"Second, of course," Papa continued, "the coffee helps give the *Chocolat* its unusual flavor. And finally—" here Papa paused and looked carefully over his shoulder as though afraid of being overheard. Then he leaned across the table and whispered, "You know how I hate waste of any kind. Well, there's always some coffee left in the pot when I'm done, so to be perfectly truthful about it, no matter what, I guess I'd pour it over the *Chocolat* anyhow."

Suddenly this struck them both as so funny that they started to laugh. They laughed, they howled, they rocked back and forth, they pounded on the table. They made such a racket that Maman came running in.

"What on earth—?" she asked, looking from one to the other of them as though they had taken leave of their senses.

Papa blew his nose and wiped his streaming eyes. "Nothing, nothing," he gasped. "Only a joke I was telling Jean-Pierre." Then, with a knowing look at Jean-Pierre, Papa quickly added, "Jean-

Pierre, your mother is a very wise woman in many ways. Why don't you take your bicycle and go for a nice ride in the fresh air?"

"Very well, Papa," said Jean-Pierre, lowering his eyes for fear that he might start laughing again. "I'll just take a short spin."

"What is to become of me?" asked Maman in a disgusted tone. "I have a memory like a sieve. Jean-Pierre, your friend, Claude, has been here several times asking for you. I saw him again through the kitchen window just now. I think we should invite him to come in."

Before Jean-Pierre could stop her, Maman went to the door and returned, followed by Claude. There he stood—as tall as ever, as handsome as ever. And yet, Jean-Pierre found he no longer minded. In fact, he was truly glad to see Claude!

Papa gave a great yawn. "Well," he said, rising from his chair, "if you two gentlemen will excuse me, I feel the need of a nap."

"And I still have a few things to do in the kitchen," said Maman.

Now that they were alone in the restaurant, Jean-Pierre and Claude felt suddenly shy. After an uncomfortable silence, Claude was the first to speak. "Where have you been?" he asked. "I've looked for you almost every day."

Jean-Pierre couldn't think how to answer Claude's question. Surely it would be unkind to tell Claude that he had been purposely avoiding him. "I, well, you see, the thing of it is, I've, I've, ah—" said Jean-Pierre, looking everywhere but at Claude.

"You've had 'something important to attend to that just wouldn't wait?' " asked Claude in a teasing voice.

"Yes, in a way," Jean-Pierre replied.

"Oh, come now," said Claude. "You don't have to be so mysterious all the time. What really keeps you so busy day after day that you always have to rush home in the middle of a bicycle ride?"

All at once, Jean-Pierre decided to tell the truth, and let Claude laugh at him if he wanted to. "I like to watch my father make a special dessert of his. It's called *Chocolat Chardin.*" Jean-Pierre said this and waited.

Claude didn't laugh. He merely looked puzzled. "I see," he said. "Well, that must be interesting—I guess," he added doubtfully.

"Yes, it was interesting today, believe me," said Jean-Pierre. "But it never would have happened if I hadn't rushed home day after day in the middle of a bicycle ride."

"There you go being mysterious again," said Claude. "*What* wouldn't have happened?"

"Look!" Jean-Pierre directed Claude. Proudly he pointed to the huge picture of the Mayor with its messages of praise for Papa and for himself. "You saw how swollen my father's cheek is? Well, he had to go to the dentist, and so I made his *Chocolat* for him," concluded Jean-Pierre, carefully leaving out the fact that Papa had made a mistake.

The expression on Claude's face was everything that Jean-Pierre could have wished. "Imagine," Claude murmured in a voice so low that Jean-

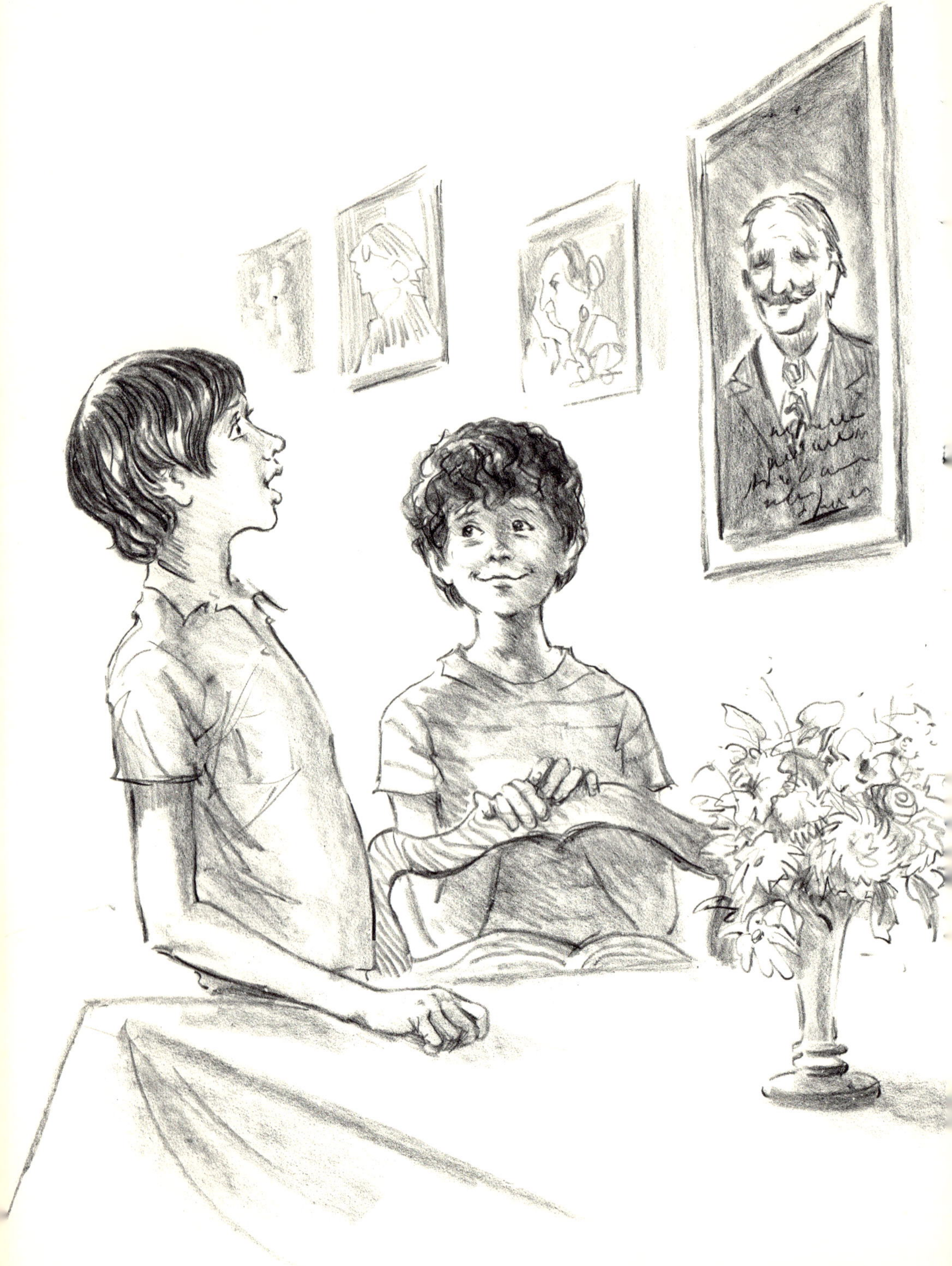

Pierre could scarcely hear it. "Only imagine! The *Mayor!*" Claude looked all around the restaurant as though searching for something to say. Finally he was struck with an idea. "Let's go for a bicycle ride," he suggested.

For a fleeting moment Jean-Pierre remembered that his bicycle was not a Comet like Claude's. But now this no longer seemed to matter, either. It was good enough.

"All right," he agreed. "But perhaps there is some *Chocolat* left over. Wouldn't you like to have some of that first? I am anxious to find out how it tastes myself."

About the Author

Amalie Sharfman is a native of Baltimore, Maryland, where she attended the Park School and Goucher College. After her marriage to a government lawyer she moved to Washington, D.C., where she continued a career in radio begun in Baltimore. She has taught nursery school at a day care center, and creative writing at Assumption College and Clark University in Worcester, Massachusetts, and at George Washington University in Washington, D.C. Mrs. Sharfman is the author of two previous books for children, *A Beagle Named Bertram* and *Mr. Peabody's Pesky Ducks*. "The experiences I have had as a result of writing them," she says, "are among the happiest I have ever had—especially the letters I received from the children I had written them for."

About the Illustrator

Lilian Obligado spent her childhood on a ranch in Argentina where there were 14,000 books. After moving with her family to the United States she was married to a diplomat attached to UNESCO, and now makes her home in Paris with her husband and small daughter. More than two dozen children's books have been enhanced by her appealing illustrations.